ORDINARY ANGELS

JOHN L. MICEK

MILFORD
HOUSE

Milford House Press
Mechanicsburg, Pennsylvania

MILFORD
HOUSE
an imprint of Sunbury Press, Inc.
Mechanicsburg, PA USA

For information about special discounts for bulk purchases, please contact Sunbury Press Orders Dept. at (855) 338-8359 or orders@sunburypress.com.

To request one of our authors for speaking engagements or book signings, please contact Sunbury Press Publicity Dept. at publicity@sunburypress.com.

ISBN: 978-1-62006-132-9 (Trade paperback)

Library of Congress Control Number:

FIRST MILFORD HOUSE PRESS EDITION: July 2019

Product of the United States of America
0 1 1 2 3 5 8 13 21 34 55

Set in Bookman Old Style
Designed by Chris Fenwick
Cover by Chris Fenwick
Edited by Chris Fenwick

Continue the Enlightenment!

As ever, to Marni, who never stopped believing – even when I did – and who convinced me that I could actually pull this off. You're the North Star.

"Naturally, we would prefer seven epiphanies a day, and an Earth not so apparently devoid of angels."

-Jim Harrison

The pain was excruciating.

I was trussed up like a Thanksgiving turkey in the back of a rented Volkswagen Passat on a stretch of Route 80 linking Fort Myers and West Palm Beach. If I were a betting man, I'd have said the bird would make out better.

My head had already bounced twice off the wheel well on the car's passenger side. The twin impacts opened a nasty gash that ran from my hairline to about my temple. And there, in the suffocating darkness, I could feel the coppery redness of my own blood flow down over my eyes and soak into my open-collared shirt.

As the blood flowed over my mouth, I spat it out to keep from retching. It was bad enough that the night was probably going to end with the sharp report of a pistol shot. I didn't want to spend whatever time I had left choking to death.

I was on my way back to Sarasota from Wellington when they grabbed me in the parking lot of a Radisson hotel at the airport in West Palm Beach. Lena was in her room, safely asleep, and I offered up a small prayer to the nearest available deity that that's where they'd left her.

When I'd kissed her good night, I smelled the citrus tang of Lena's perfume and the gentle, flowery notes of the soap she always used.

But I was tired, and we'd argued.

"See you in the morning," she muttered, as we kissed be-grudgingly.

The hard rubber of an extension cord bit into my wrists, leaving my hands numb. My shoulders were stretched tight, and there was a good chance that one of them had been dis-located when the Passat lurched violently over what I'd as-sumed to be the curb in the hotel parking lot.

I couldn't be sure how much time had passed. I'd blacked out at least once and the stifling air made it difficult to focus. "Breathe, Flynn," I told myself. "Just breathe. You'll figure a way out of this."

The trunk's emergency release latch lay agonizingly just out of reach.

Some German engineer had thoughtfully decided to coat the piece of angled plastic in that pale green glow-in-the-dark goop they put on kid's Halloween toys. Good to know that the guys at Volkswagen's world headquarters paid such attention to detail.

In the dark of the trunk, the latch was a beacon. But it was also an annoying reminder of the bleakness of my current state of affairs.

Another bump. My head caromed off the roof of the trunk. There was a sickening thud, and, overcome by nausea and the heat, my world went black yet again.

I was awakened ... how much later ... an hour ... ten minutes ... I couldn't be sure. I felt two strong pairs of arms drag me from the trunk and I sputtered as they splashed cold water on my face. There was a flash of pain in my knees as they collided with the pavement.

I landed face first, scraping my cheek against the gravel. There was a crushed cigarette butt, ringed by a woman's lipstick, just an inch or so from my right eye.

As I was violently pulled upright, I found myself in the parking lot of a strip mall that fallen on black days. The boarded-up windows of a long-forgotten department store chain stared forlornly into the dark of the parking lot.

The crème brulee smell in the air probably meant we were somewhere around Lake Okeechobee. This part of south Florida lay in the heart of the state's sugar industry.

Down here, they started planting sugar cane in August and stopped around January. Twelve or eighteen months later, the crops were harvested after a controlled burning. And that accounted for the French restaurant smell.

When they were done, planters were left with the raw sugar so beloved by habitués of the nation's finer coffeehouses. They were also left with two major by-products: blackstrap molasses and a substance called bagasse that helps make plastic.

Besides cakes and cookies, the molasses also finds its way into cattle feed and, eventually, rum

The thought of rum felt pretty good. If this was to be the end, then I at least wanted to go out feeling all right.

"I don't suppose you have any Captain Morgan?" I asked hoarsely as one of my captors, a big guy with a pockmarked face and forearms the size of hams thrust me back to my knees. I grunted at the impact and felt gravel bite into my skin. As I looked up, I could see flies buzzing in the sodium lights overhead. At this hour, the windows of homes across the street were darkened and even the criminals had gone to sleep.

It wasn't much cooler outside than it had been in the trunk. Even in March, the air had a cloying moistness that caused your clothes to cling to your body. The blood flowing from my head wound mingled with sweat. There was no moon.

My captors had formed a half-circle around me. Hamhocks stood at the far-right side of the crescent. He was flanked by a surfer-looking dude with limp blonde hair. He had the kind of skinny build that was wiry -- but not weak. Next to him stood a red-haired guy with a friendly, Irish face that didn't conceal the cruel line of his jagged mouth.

"What'd you say?" Red-Hair asked me.

"Captain Morgan," I asked again, my voice a hoarse whisper. "I don't suppose you have any Captain Morgan?"

Red-Hair smiled grimly.

"Buddy," he said. "Where you're going, the bar's always open."

The half-moon of assailants closed tighter around me. From his pocket, Red-Hair drew something that glinted menacingly in the sodium lights.

"This won't end well, is it?" I asked.

"Not for you," Red-Hair said.

CHAPTER 1

It began with a story. The way they always do.

I was working late cops on a hot night in July. It was just before ten o'clock, and all around me, the city desk of the Harrisburg Banner buzzed with life.

The newsroom, on the building's second floor, was a low rectangle with all the charm of a nuclear waste dump.

Fifty years ago, the Banner had been one of Pennsylvania's great newspapers. Its family owners, whose names you'd recognize if I told you, made their fortunes in the anthracite coalfields around Hazleton and Wilkes-Barre.

After what I supposed had been one too many viewings of "Citizen Kane," the family owners had decided to style themselves after the newspaper barons of the early 20th Century.

They'd turned The Banner into a scrappy tabloid that covered crime and politics with the same zeal that it covered baseball and football.

There'd been at least two ownership changes since those early glory years.

That's when The Banner regularly took home a fistful of awards and even nailed a Pulitzer to its trophy room wall.

Now, the paper was a broadsheet owned by bean counters in Chicago. And it was just one holding in a vast media empire that also included television and radio stations, magazines and a minor league baseball team. The jokes about minor league newspapers also abounded.

The family owners had a building named after them in downtown Harrisburg that was now in the same state of disrepair as their prized newspaper.

The repeated shifts in ownership had thrust The Banner into an identity crisis from which it had never really recovered. The old-timers still liked to talk about those far-away salad days. But they were as yellowed as the framed front-pages outside the publisher's mahogany-paneled suite of offices -- and they were about as believable.

Circulation had dwindled from a high of around 200,000 daily copies to just a shade over 100,000 on Sundays.

Advertisers were deserting for the Internet. And, now, like most newspapers, The Banner was struggling to redefine itself to a mostly suburban readership that barely had the time to pay attention to its product.

For reporters, The Banner was a great place to start or end a career.

The living in Harrisburg was cheap, though the city was slowly gentrifying. New and converted lofts were sprouting up all over the city's Midtown neighborhood.

All were an easy walk to a resurgent central market and the farm-to-table restaurant next door.

Downtown, there were some decent bars and restaurants that filled with young partiers from three surrounding counties every weekend.

And because Harrisburg was Pennsylvania's Capital City, there was no shortage of stories about the city's largest employer: state government.

All that bureaucracy made for easy pickings for the ambitious -- but those who were good enough got out as soon as they could.

That didn't explain me -- but more about that in a while.

Of course, The Banner still made money, but not nearly as much money as it used to make. The paper's owners were still struggling to adjust to the shift to digital advertising, which would never be as lucrative as the huge print spreads it had trained its advertisers to buy.

In the city room, the neglect showed.

At one end of the room, a bank of windows looked out over Market Street, a parking lot, and the numbing edifice of the city's central post office.

At the far end of the rectangle, underneath a bank of fluorescent lights that dangled from a drop ceiling oozing with asbestos and God knows what other toxins, a trio of sports reporters, telephone headsets crushed against their ears, took bar league softball scores that no one, probably not even the players, would care about in 24 hours.

"So, it was Midtown Marauders, 5, Larry's Uptown, 4?" one grizzled veteran, his glasses pushed down his nose, demanded as he pecked, two-fingered, at the keyboard below him.

At the other end of the rectangle, nearest to the windows, copy editors, some of them lifers with gray hair, haggled over the front-page headlines.

Could they use the word "Slammed" in a four-column headline in a front-page story about three teenagers killed in a car crash?

The reporters were sandwiched between the copy desk and the sports department by the deserted features desk.

Save for a few stragglers, the section of The Banner that produced stories about gardening, food, health, and pop culture was empty.

The reporters' desks spread out along a vertical plane from the "T" of the copy desk. At the terminus of the "T", a bank of low filing cabinets served as the de facto border between news and features. My desk was about two-thirds of the way down on the left as you looked across the room from the windows. Reporters were separated by cloth-lined, half-partitions that were just low enough to shout over.

Facing me, a young reporter, fresh out of school, named Melanie Goslin, struggled with a story about a local planning board.

Her thick auburn hair fell in waves over her shoulders and bangs dangled in her eyes as she peered intently at the computer screen in front of her. The reflection cast a pale glow against her oval-framed glasses. She was talented. I gave her two years at most.

The desk to my immediate left was empty. To my right, a mid-career reporter named Brent Vernet put the finishing touches on a story about that night's boisterous city council meeting.

The council was considering a citywide public smoking ban that year. And since the downtown district was lined with trendy restaurants and bars, it was a big story.

Well, big for Harrisburg anyway.

I glanced over the wall at Vernet's computer screen and winced.

"You sure about that lead, Brent?" I asked him, a mischievous smile playing at the corners of my mouth.

Vernet looked up and made a face at me.

"It's an anti-smoking story, Sean," he said. "Gotta' work the 'huffing and puffing' reference in there somewhere."

"Could have been worse," I said. "How?" Vernet returned.

"I'm really not sure," I told him.

I'd also been monitoring the police scanner that sat perched atop three decaying phone books at the upper-right corner of my desk.

There'd been a car crash on Cameron Street about three blocks from the office. It had been uneventful until now, and the scanner chatter was filled with the usual numb talk until I heard that fateful word:

"Fatal accident."

"Drake!" I shouted to the night city editor. Eddie Drake was a frazzled guy prone to wrinkled shirts, clashing pants and a talent for pedantry.

But he was also one of the best editors I'd ever worked with.

He looked up.

"Yeah?" he asked.

"That crash on Cameron Street?" I said. "It's a fatal. Think I'll check it out."

"I can't even understand what you're still doing here," Drake barked as he jerked his head towards the door.

"Go," he said. "I'll have a photog meet you there."

I grabbed a notebook and two pens. I slung my press-pass around my neck – it read Sean Flynn -- and headed out into the hot July night.

CHAPTER 2

The two-block walk went quickly. And when I got there, Cameron Street was barricaded for a three-block area that started at its intersection with Market Street to the south and ran until Goodwill Drive to the north.

A quartet of Harrisburg police cruisers, their dome lights flashing in the heavy darkness, had been pressed into ser vice to keep away the curious. Two of the blue-and-yellow striped cruisers were parked nose-to-nose at each end of the crime scene. A single officer stood in front of each.

I walked up from Market and hung a left. A burly officer shone a flashlight in my face.

"Evening, Phil," I said, recognizing the fortyish cop barring my path. His pointed cap was jammed down tightly over his blonde crew cut. He hadn't shaved.

He nodded at me.

"Stay out of the way, Sean," he said as I strode past him.

After 15 years in the news trade, most of them as a police re- porter, I had learned long ago not to get underfoot at a crime scene.

The cops appreciated the respect. And it paid off in stories. My father, a former district attorney in Illinois, would have been proud.

Cameron Street was one of the city's main north-south arteries.

It started in the north near the state Farm Show complex and ran for six miles into the struggling borough of Steelton, where its name changed to Front Street.

For most of its length, Cameron Street was lined with factories, industrial sites and a giant scrap yard that gave off an eerie glow in the nighttime hours as giant spotlights flickered off the ghostly remains of compacted cars.

There was a public housing project halfway down Cameron Street's northern extreme, not far from where it terminated near the Farm Show.

Like a lot of urban Harrisburg, it had its fair share of crime. And not long ago, an eight-year-old boy had been caught in the crossfire there between two warring gangs.

He'd been on his way to a convenience store to buy some candy with the money his grandmother had given him, we learned later. They'd left him where he'd fallen.

The wreck sat roughly in the middle of the barricaded zone. The little, black Honda Accord had gone off the road in the northbound lane, just across the street from a popular brewpub, where it had slammed into a utility pole. The force of the impact had cut a malevolent vee through the center of the hood.

And there was the expected spider-web shatter pattern across the windshield from where the victim's head had slammed into the heavy glass.

The victim – whoever he or she was – was already long gone by the time I got there. Harrisburg Hospital was only a few blocks away along Front Street near the river, and the city's ambulance corps was known for its fast response times. If the driver hadn't survived, chances were good that he or she was already headed for a slab in the morgue.

A cop I knew, Marty Herman, was running the scene. He was as solid as a fireplug.

Marty had boxed amateur for a while, picking up bouts at the Saturday night fights under the cupolas at the Masonic Temple uptown near the high school.

He'd had a shot at going pro. But Marty spent too much time getting knocked down.

At just a shade over five-foot-ten, he didn't have the reach or the size to stand toe-to-toe with the bigger guys. He'd boxed super-middleweight and tipped the scales at a spare168 pounds in his prime.

At 35, he'd gone a little soft, and probably weighed something closer to 185.

But he was still one of the toughest guys I knew.

"Marty," I called to him across the street. Herman looked up from the wreck, followed the sound of my voice, and his eyes gradually settled on me. He nodded.

"In a minute, Flynn," he said, and went back to inspecting the wreck.

A dented white tow-truck pulled up to the scene, and a short Hispanic man in torn jeans and a sleeveless T-shirt hopped out of the cab, and without a word, began setting up the hooks and chains needed to pull the car from the scene.

While the wrecker driver set about his task, Marty Herman broke away from two or other officers working on the car. He gave instructions to the two young cops, who nodded and returned to work.

He crossed the street in four or five energetic strides and stepped onto the sidewalk where I was standing.

As he did, he exchanged greetings with another young officer, who was using one of those single-wheeled measuring tools to pace off the distance from the stoplight at the top of Market Street to the impact point. The working cop didn't look up as Marty greeted him.

"Hot tonight," he said, mopping his forehead with a handkerchief he drew from his back pocket. He cast a longing glance at the brewpub behind us. "How are you, Sean?"

We shook hands. I winced at the grip as Marty squeezed with one of his big bear paws.

I followed his glance and fished a notebook from my back-pocket. "I'll buy you a round later, Marty. Whaddya got?"

"A car crash," he said, grinning just a little.

"You're hilarious," I shot back. "It's after ten, and I'm forty-five minutes from deadline."

"All right, all right," he threw his hands in the air in mock-surrender. "You've got me, Woodward. What do you need?

"Lay it out for me," I told him. "Who's the victim?"

Herman nodded seriously and spat into the street.

"No name yet. We're still waiting to notify the family, understand? What I can tell you: a Caucasian male in his twenties. He was headed north along Cameron shortly before 10 p.m. when his vehicle left the roadway and struck a PPL pole in the northbound shoulder. We're assuming the victim was killed on impact. We're awaiting the results of the toxicology tests to see if alcohol was involved."

I scribbled furiously, nodding as I got caught up in my notes.

"Passenger?" I asked, without looking up.

"Not that we know of," Marty said, glancing across the street as the wrecker pulled a U-turn on Cameron, then a quick right onto Market.

Probably headed to the police impound garage on Cranberry Alley, I thought. "The lab guys still have to go over the car."

"Witnesses?"

Marty looked at me like I'd suggested that the sun rose in the west.

"Of course not," I said. "Any idea how fast he was going?"

"Reconstruction guys are still working on that," he returned. "But, hell, Sean. You saw the car. He was going fast enough to make an accordion out of the vehicle."

We both looked across the street as the accident crews began to clean up.

Soon, it would look like nothing had even happened here. But some people would know forever.

"One thing I can't figure out, though," Marty Herman said, as we gazed across the street together.

He pushed his cap back on his forehead, exposing a shock of sweat-tangled black hair.

"What's that?"

"It's a car accident, right?" he asked. "You been doing this a while. What's missing here?"

Either because it was late or because the oppressive humidity had made me tired and cranky, I wasn't much in the mood for playing detective.

"Christ, I don't know, Marty," I said testily, casting a worried glance at my watch as it ticked down to our first edition deadline. "What's missing?"

"Guy like you can't figure it out, there's no hope for any of us," Herman joked.

"C'mon, Marty, it's getting late."

"No skid-marks," Marty Herman curtly said as he turned away toward his cruiser.

I stood there, just looking at the street for a little while after he drove away. Then I took my cellphone out of my pocket and called in the story.

By Sean Flynn Banner Staff Writer

HARRISBURG _ City police are investigating a fatal accident that claimed the life of an as-yet-unidentified motorist late last night.

Police said the driver was traveling in the northbound lane near 50 North Cameron around 9:30 p.m. when the car left the roadway and struck a PPL utility pole on the sidewalk.

Harrisburg City Police told The Banner last night that the identity of the driver would be released pending notification of family.

It was not immediately clear whether there was a passenger in the vehicle, a 2017 Honda Accord. Police declined to comment on the likely cause of the crash or whether alcohol was involved.

sean.flynn@bannernews.com (717) 885-6628

I was having an early lunch downtown at the Twin Fountains Diner. And it was just after eleven o'clock when my cell phone rang.

The diner had been done up to look like someone's idea of 1950s kitsch. Old forty-fives were glued to the stainless-steel border that ran above the narrow pass-through to the kitchen. The booths were polished chrome with red leatherette benches. The benches in booths matched the padding on the stools at the counter where I sat. The floor was patterned with hexagonal tiles in an alternating pattern of black-and-white.

It was busy for a Wednesday. State employees and legislative staffers sat shoulder-to-shoulder at the counter.

The line for tables ran four-deep at the door, and waitresses, dressed like the touring company for "Grease" worked the narrow aisles, balancing trays heavy with food above their heads as their ponytails bounced along behind them.

On the speakers above my head, Dion's "Runaround Sue," blared. I could have done without the kitsch. But a good diner was hard to find. And it was one of the few places in town where I could ask for an egg cream without someone looking at me like I'd just fallen from space.

Though I was still tired, it had been a good morning.

The day had started with a quick run along the Susquehanna River, which stretched long, brown and hot along the city's western border, cleaving industrialized Dauphin County from its largely rural and suburban neighbor, Cumberland County on the opposing shore. The distances that separated the two counties often seemed more than geographic.

Cumberland was, well, the snootier of the two counties, home to affluent suburbanites and old Pennsylvania farmers who looked down their noses at a city that was becoming more diverse by the day.

It had been cool for July. Harrisburg in summer was often unmercifully hot and humid. It was a cloying, soak-your-shirt heat that shared more in common with its comrade states to the south than with its friends to the north.

Psychologically, the city had a lot in common with the American south.

Outside of York and Gettysburg, Harrisburg was one of Pennsylvania's southernmost cities. And if you talked to locals, sometimes you caught that upward lilt at the end of their syllables that you also heard in places like Maryland and Virginia.

The Susquehanna River had been one of the main selling points when I moved to Harrisburg from California eight years ago.

Riverfront Park was a well-manicured oasis lined with old mansions and lovingly maintained row homes that were routinely flooded during the winter thaws.

Even though the prospect of thousands of dollars in property damage had been something of a deterrent, I'd nonetheless moved into a 100-year-old rowhouse at the far end of the city's Shipoke district. It was tranquil and leafy and populated by artists, working professionals, and the occasional state lawmaker.

The neighbors were friendly -- even if they probably secretly thought that the presence of a reporter in their midst was driving down their property values.

There was a cheap restaurant just up the street from my house. I ate there frequently. The waitresses knew my name. And Sam, the owner, a burly Greek whose arms were crisscrossed with tattoos, let me keep a couple of good bottles of red wine behind the counter.

We'd shared more than a few of them during long dinners that usually ended with Sam telling rambling stories about life in the old country.

He was from Pittsburgh, I later learned. But that hadn't diminished the charm of his drunken tales.

My phone buzzed again, more insistently, it seemed, wrenching me away from a turkey club and a chocolate egg cream.

"Flynn," I answered.

"I got a name on our guy," Marty Herman said without identifying himself. In the background, there was a beeping noise. Like all police phone calls, we were being recorded.

"Marty," I protested through a full mouth. "I'm having lunch here."

"Ohhhh ... sorry ... if you're too busy, Mr. Big-Shot Reporter, I could always call the television stations and put you at the bottom of my call-sheet."

"Gimme what you got," I shot back, as I fished a notebook and pen out of a battered leather satchel at my feet. I pushed that day's copy of the New York Times out of my way to make space on the counter.

"Peter Andre. Age 26. Lived in the 2300 block of North Front Street -- y'know, the big high-rise that overlooks the river?"

"Un-hunh."

"Date of birth: June 5, 1992. Hometown, Elizabethtown, Lancaster County. Not married. No kids."

"What else?" I asked, wolfing down a bite of sandwich and washing it down with a sip from the tall egg cream beside it.

"Worked on the Hill for a Democratic state senator from Philadelphia," Marty continued, reading from his notes.

Behind him, I could hear the bustle of the squad room, and an explosion of laughter.

"Who?"

"Guy named J. Clarence McGeehan. He was his chief-of-staff."

I let out a low, long whistle.

"That a big deal?" Marty asked.

"Yep," I said through another mouthful of sandwich. "The guy's the second-most powerful Democrat in the state behind, maybe, the governor."

"Humph," Marty said. "All well and good, but you haven't asked me the cause of death yet, have you, Scoop?"

I exhaled heavily.

"No, Marty, I haven't," I said. "But I'm guessing that it wasn't the speed of the car that killed him, so much as it was the sudden stop at the end."

At his end of the phone, Marty laughed grimly.

"You'd like to think so, wouldn't you?" he said.

"What was it, Marty?"

"Gunshot. Single gunshot. Straight through. Surprised we didn't see it earlier. But there wasn't a shot through the windshield or any other obvious entry points through the car," he said.

"There's more," Marty said. "It gets worse?"

"Yeah. He was shot in the side, Sean. You know what that means, don't you?"

He didn't need to tell me.

"There was someone else in the car," I said.

"Uh-hunh," Marty said. "Or, he'd been shot before he started driving."

I signaled the waitress for the check.

CHAPTER 4

When I got to the office, The Banner newsroom was bustling in the way that only newspapers bustle when a big story hits.

There was a palpable energy in the air that was magnified by the clatter of fingertips banging away on laptop keyboards, telephone chatter and the unmistakable musk of adrenaline that hung in the air.

Everything was moving faster. Reporters zipped down the pathways between cubicles. Editors darted in and out of meetings. And photographers, already an over-caffeinated bunch, to begin with, assembled their gear and headed for the doors.

I'd tapped out a quick story on my iPhone as I walked the four or five blocks from the Fountain to the office.

Ignoring the lunchtime pedestrian traffic, I cradled my cellphone on one shoulder and let the day City Editor, a scrawny guy with a big voice named Vic Young, in on the story.

Within a couple of minutes, my story was on the Banner's Web page, and the online unit had already sent out an emergency update to our e-mail subscribers.

Young was standing at my desk when I arrived.

His thinning hair was combed over with a part that started just above his right ear and it swooped over the top of his round head, creating a blanket of hair that even Donald Trump would have envied.

He peered at me through rimless glasses.

I put my satchel down on my desk and pulled up my email to check for new messages.

"Nice job," said Young, a hardcore news junkie who'd come to The Banner from a newspaper in upstate New York.

At 45, he was unmarried or was so dedicated to his work that he gave off the impression of being unmarried. Nothing but the story came first with him.

I'd seen his type before. Every newsroom has at least one editor who gets giddy with joy when they hear about a fire. Young was that guy.

I opened a desk drawer and fished out a fresh notebook and a couple of pens.

My laptop beeped at me, letting me know that a new email, with a headshot of Peter Andre attached to it, had arrived.

The face that stared back at me was young and untested. The eyes were clear, and his face was framed by a thatch of closely-cropped blonde hair.

In the photo, Peter Andre smiled confidently, like he had all the time in the world.

"Thanks," I told him without looking up as I stuffed my booty into my satchel. "What's the plan?"

"You're on this one with Mike Vivian," Young said, referring to our political reporter, who was too fond, for my taste, of the sound of his own voice.

He was famed for writing long, ponderous columns that his sources adored, but left most of the readership scratching their heads. I hadn't read to the bottom of one of them in years.

I grimaced.

"I know," he said. "But Vivian's got the contacts at the Capitol that you don't have. And he can nail down everything there is to know about this guy in a couple of hours."

"Fine, fine," I said. Vivian and I had worked together in the past. I found him a bit overbearing as a colleague. But it wasn't a fatal flaw. There had been far worse.

"What do you want from me?" I asked.

"You'll be writing the main bar. Vivian will feed from the Capitol. We've got Melanie in Elizabethtown trying to track down family or friends for a sider. You're back to Cameron Street. The cops said there weren't any witnesses. But somebody always sees something," he said.

I nodded in assent. My phone rang. I ignored it.

"You find anything," Young continued. "Call it in, and we'll get someone to take rewrite and slap it up on the Web as soon as they can. The big guns are going whole-hog for this thing, and they've promised continuing coverage that's gonna' keep pace with the TV people."

"All right, all right," I said. "I got it."

In a lot of ways, the advent of the Web had been a godsend for newspapers. No longer did reporters have to wait until the next day to get a story out.

Thanks to the miracle of the web, breaking stories could be posted right away. For hard news junkies, it was a dream come true.

But it also put a lot of pressure on beat reporters to deliver copy while they were tracking down a big story.

The news business was becoming more and more futuristic all the time – as my smartphone attested.

But in some ways, we were also reverting to the 19th Century days of the penny papers where the emphasis was put on lurid crime news above all else.

Some of the older guys groused. Our younger reporters, already computer savvy, went along with it because it was all they had ever known.

Me, I liked it too. There was nothing I hated more than getting beat on a story.

"I'd start at the brewpub if I were you," Young said, leaning against the low partition that separated my desk from Vernet's.

"Just what I was thinking," I said.

I shouldered my satchel and began to walk away from my desk.

"Gonna' be awful hard to find witnesses if the cops couldn't dig them up, Vic," I said over my shoulder.

Young smiled.

"You're starting at a bar, Sean. I have faith in you."

Then I was down the stairs and out into the street and walking through the unforgiving midday July sun toward the Cameron Street Brewing Co.

CHAPTER 5

The upstairs bar at the Cameron Street Brewing Co. was dark and cool, and a welcome respite from a day that was quickly becoming blast furnace hot.

I pushed open the double doors that led to the second floor and was hit with a whoosh of air conditioning that blew my hair back from my forehead and froze the sweat that pooled in the small of my back.

I'd stopped to talk to a pair of hostesses on the way up. The brewery was divided into a 150-seat restaurant that took up most of the first-floor downstairs and the sports pub upstairs The restaurant walls were exposed brick and dotted with the standard array of faux-Irish bar plaques that the owners no doubt hoped would confer some sort of ersatz Old World charm on the place.

Funny thing about Americans: we couldn't wait to be independent, but we were still in love with the trappings of the Empire. That was okay with me. I loved the original "Alfie."

The floors were the same polished oak as the tabletops. The ceilings were high and vaulted and the place was deafening when it was busy -- which was most of the time.

A pair of plate glass windows on the building's western front looked out over the broad expanse of Cameron Street. And a pair of four-seaters was planted in each window. It was hard to believe that, at 10 p.m., when the restaurant was still open, that a stray patron, waitress or even a busboy hadn't borne witness to Peter Andre's final moments.

The restaurant's north wall was glass and steel and looked into the brewery section.

The standard arrangement of pipes and giant tanks stared back. A couple of workers in white lab coats moved among the tanks. They chatted briefly and then moved on.

Years ago, before it gentrified, the building had been an actual brewery and even produced a lawnmower beer that approached drinkable. I hadn't been around in those days. But those who had told me the beer wasn't bad.

The hostesses regarded me with studied indifference as I thrust business cards into their reluctant palms. They didn't answer any questions.

As I left, I told them to feel free to call if they remembered anything or knew someone who could help. I didn't think I'd hear from either of them.

Upstairs, the sports pub was mostly empty, save for a few professional drinkers already well into their heads for the day. A trio of them sat on three sides of the hollow square of a bar that was situated in the back of the long room.

The front half was given over to pool tables, a few dart boards, a jukebox well-stocked with utterly atrocious 70s AOR rock, and a stage that hosted local bands.

I'd been here the week before with two guys from the sports department.

We sat at the bar until the wee hours of Saturday morning listening to an Uncle Tupelo-style alt.country band as we got sloppy on Old Fashioneds.

When I woke in my clothes the next morning with my tongue arc-welded to the roof of my mouth and a mariachi band playing in my head, I realized, to my horror, that I'd been foolish enough to actually drive myself home.

The bartender, a tall guy with chiseled features and an athletic build, was drying off highball glasses as I entered. He nodded at me and went back to work.

I walked slowly through the nearly empty sports pub and took a seat at the top of the square next to a video-poker machine.

My back was to the door. An elevator, a dartboard and the doors to each restroom were on my immediate left. A bank of windows that overlooked a state office building lined the wall to my right.

The bartender put down a highball glass and slid down the bar to me.

He smiled through crooked teeth and a face burned deep red by too much time in the sun.

"Afternoon," I said, leaning on the bar, and sliding my satchel to the seat next to me.

"Good afternoon, sir. Welcome to Cameron Street. What can I get you?"

I glanced in the direction of the three professionals.

"A couple of hours too early to start," I said. "Just give me a Diet with some lemon. I could also use some information." The bartender's eyes narrowed as I pulled out my press credential. and flashed it at him.

"Sean Flynn with The Banner," I said. "Were you working last night?"

The barkeep moved quickly to the soda gun and splashed some Diet Pepsi into a tall glass that was three-quarters full of ice.

He reached beneath the bar into the fruit tray and slid a lemon wedge onto the lip of the glass and popped a skinny stirrer straw into the glass. He grabbed a napkin, slid back down the bar, and set the drink in front of me.

"This about the car crash?" he said. "I didn't' see anything."

I took a meditative sip of my drink. The soda hit the back of my throat, and I felt it slide down and splash in my stomach.

"Maybe you didn't," I said. "Does it make a difference if I don't use your name?"

"It might," he said.

"How much for the Diet?"

"Two-fifty."

I put ten on the two-fifty and told him to keep it. The barkeep's face brightened.

"Most people aren't that smart," he said.

I nodded.

"Lucky for you, I'm not 'most people,'" I said, as I pulled up Peter Andre's headshot on my phone. "Ever seen this guy in here before?" I asked.

The barkeep stared passively at the photo.

In it, Peter Andre had that old-before-his-time look that I'd seen in the faces of the ambitious kids I had known as an undergraduate.

When that picture was taken four years ago, Andre's eyes were already on the prize: a badly paying job as a legislative staffer that he probably thought he could eventually parlay into a gig as a political consultant or lobbyist while he positioned himself for a run for office himself someday.

In Harrisburg, it was a common storyline, and the bars on Second Street around the Capitol were filled with hundreds of Peter Andre's of both sexes during the post-Happy Hour rush.

Kids like him didn't punch the clock. They'd stay at the office. When the Legislature was in session, they'd stay even longer, order in sandwiches, and get about, they thought, God's work.

The barkeep's forehead creased in concentration, and then a slow smile spread across his face.

"Oh yeah, this guy," he said.

"You know him?"

"Pretty Pete," the bartender grinned. "He was in here two, three nights a week sometimes. Always ordered an Absolut and tonic. Two limes. He was always on the prowl."

I nodded and scribbled some notes.

"'Pretty Pete?" I asked.

The bartender laughed mirthlessly.

"Nickname. He was always done up to the nines whenever he came in. Good suits, probably custom jobs like Indochino. Same with the shirts and ties. Classic preppy look, you know?"

I inspected my own outfit of khaki trousers, loafers, and a blue button-down from J.Crew. Yeah, it was something I knew a little bit about.

The bartender continued

"I knew what he did for a living too," he said, reaching to wipe some stubby rocks glasses from the bar sink beneath him. "No way he could afford it unless he bought all his stuff at outlets."

I wrote some more. He was talking now. No reason to interrupt. Worst thing you can do with an interview is to interrupt someone when they're on a roll.

I nodded, as an indication that he should continue.

"Usually, he was in here with a different woman or ended the night with one he'd picked up. The other night, he was in here with a tall, strawberry blonde. Didn't catch her name. Willowy, but in shape."

He caught himself and looked at me nervously.

"You're not using my name, right?" he asked.

"Have I asked you your name?" I retorted. He looked relieved.

"Had a hell of row in here, those two," the barkeep said, picking up the tale, and warming to it as he got deeper into it. "Not sure over what. It was obvious they'd known each other for a while. There was a familiarity with the way they hung on each other. Every so often, she'd whisper in his ear and kiss him on the cheek."

"You catch any of it?" I asked and tapped my glass for a refill. Muscle memory kicked in as the bartender went through the same series of motions he had when he'd drawn my drink. He kept talking.

"Not much. It sounded like it had something to do with money."

"Don't they all?" I said, remembering arguments over cash with an ex-wife who no longer spoke to me.

The barkeep laughed.

"Sure, seems that way," he said. "All I remember the lady saying was, 'I can't believe you blew all of it.'" Then she grabbed her coat and purse and stormed out."

"He go after her?"

"If you'd seen her, pal, you would have too," the barkeep said. "But he made sure to drain his glass before he left."

"A perfectionist," I said. "I like that."

"Pete's the guy who died in the accident, right?"

"Yeah," I said. "It was over pretty quick."

The bartender grimaced.

"Too bad. Too damned bad."

"Why?"

The bartender moved to the center of the bar and began wiping down the rail bottles.

"He was a damned good tipper."

The barkeep turned away and didn't say goodbye as I shouldered my satchel and headed for the door.

CHAPTER 6

A pair of conversations with two guys in the auto-body shop across Cameron Street from the brewpub didn't yield much more information. The shop had been closed when the crash took place. The two guys working complained good-naturedly about the television reporters who double-parked their microwave trucks in the short driveway that fed directly into traffic.

I didn't have much more luck at the bodega at the top of Cameron near its intersection with Market Street. Nor did I commit any journalism when I tried to interview Andre's neighbors at the utterly anonymous apartment com- plex he had last called home.

I left 45 minutes later, burdened with the usual "He was quiet, kept to himself," answers I got from the handful of people who were home.

The leasing agent, who snapped her gum at me and drummed her brightly painted fingernails on her desktop, told me he always made his rent. What I knew so far was pretty good though.

Peter Andre was a young, up-and-comer, working for one of the state's most prominent and powerful legislators. He was educated, like most Pennsylvanians, at Penn State.

He was fond of partying and had been seen having an argument over cash with a strawberry blonde on the night he died.

Add that to whatever Mike Vivian gleaned from his chats at the Capitol, and lace in some of Melanie Goslin's feed from Elizabethtown, and you had something approximating a decent story.

Still, that didn't account for the gunshot wound and the lack of skid marks at the accident scene. But that was something for the cops to figure out.

Solving crimes was, most of the time, their jobs. Sketching out all the details that make a life – no matter how mundane – that was ours.

And after nearly two decades in the news business, I'd like to think that I'd gotten pretty good at it.

As I walked back to the office, I tried to imagine Melanie, intense and bookish, knocking on the front door of Peter Andre's family home and asking for an interview. She was fresh out of Northwestern's J-School.

And I wondered if she had spent any time standing at the bottom of the driveway, plucking up her courage, like we all did that first time before she made the long walk to the front stoop and the doorbell.

It was a rite of passage for all of us: the interview with the victim's family.

Mine was seventeen years gone. And I still remembered the aluminum taste of fear in my mouth and the palms that were so sweaty that I could barely hold onto the pen and notebook I was carrying.

I'm pretty sure the victim's family – she was a 16-year-old girl, kidnapped, raped, and then left in a car trunk – felt sorry for me.

I remembered sitting in their tiny living room in an industrial section of Winston-Salem, North Carolina, while they pulled down pictures of 'Their Nadine,' – that's what they called her, and told me stories about her barely formed life.

I had excused myself when the news started, and a meticulously coiffed anchor started talking about the "Sex Murder," in the city's West End.

The family, a mother, father, and two brothers didn't look up from the television as I shut the front door quietly behind me.

Conversations like that never got any easier. And I wondered how Melanie had done with hers.

Two voicemails, one from Marty Herman, another from an old friend from Orange County, were waiting for me when I got back to my desk.

I logged the call from my buddy and picked up the phone and called the Harrisburg Police Department.

There were two, long rings, and then Marty picked up.

"I really shouldn't be engaging in information-sharing with a law enforcement agency," I told him after he barked a brief, and mostly obscene, salutation. "Might make people think that we're de facto agents of the state."

"That's true," Herman said through a mouthful of something. "But then, I might never talk to you again. And then, where would you be?"

"Excellent rejoinder," I told him. "Your repartee sparkles. Have you been taking lessons?"

"I'm busy, Flynn," Herman said. "Whaddya want?"

"Same ground rules as always, Marty," I said. "I tell you what I know. You tell me what you know."

"Tell me," he said.

And I did. When I was finished, I heard the rustle of waxed paper and listened to Marty chew thoughtfully.

"Donut?" I asked.

"Croissant."

"Yuppie bastard," I said. "Your turn."

"Toxicology tests came back," he said. "Our boy was positively pickled. Had a blood-alcohol level two times the legal limit. It's amazing he was able to drive at all."

"That all you found?"

Marty chewed some more.

Around me, The Banner newsroom hummed along. Editors shouted back and forth. Reporters pecked away at their laptops.

The fluorescent lights above my head buzzed and then flashed. The drop ceilings, for all I knew, probably belched more toxins into the overly conditioned air.

"There was more," Marty Herman said.

"There always is," I said.

"Tox tests found evidence of cocaine in his system. And, they found evidence of sexual activity. Looks like your boy went out high and happy before he died," he said.

"There are worse ways," I said.

"You and me, we've seen most of them, Sean," he said.

"I know."

We hung up. And I started to write.

It was after eight o'clock by the time the copy desk had had its way with my story and Mike Vivian, and I had had the usual bout of disagreements over how much of his pristine copy was going to be left on the cutting room floor.

As was his custom, Vivian had written way too much, and wanted me to use most everything he'd given me.

"Mike, we've only got twenty-two inches," I told him, running a hand through my brown hair and wiping the early traces of sleep from my eyes.

Vivian, who was at least a head taller than me, peered down from over his glasses.

His blonde hair was thinning at the temples. Paired with his gaunt face and washed-out blue eyes, he had the look of a well-read funeral director.

His tie was askew, and the underarms of his light blue-button down were ringed with perspiration.

"But this is good stuff, Sean," he said. "And it's something that the people in this town need to know."

I peered at the screen and the torrent of copy and shook my head.

"No, Mike," I told him. "No one cares if this guy made your Top Ten poll of the Most Influential Legislative Staffers for the last three years running. Your sources maybe care about that. But the readers don't."

Vivian heaved a huge sigh.

"Use whatever the hell you want, Flynn," he said, stalking off to his desk. As he left, Vivian trailed a wake of indignation and B.O.

Melanie Goslin's copy, on the other hand, was tight, clear and to-the-point. She'd scored the interview with the victim's family.

More, she'd scored an interview with Andre's fiancée, a graduate of both Lancaster Catholic High School and Millersville State University.

She was twenty-three and had never lived more than an hour from home. There were plenty of young people like that that in central Pennsylvania.

Even better, the photo we had of her showed a clear-eyed brunette.

Peter Andre had been spotted in the Cameron Street brew-pub arguing with a willowy blonde.

And they'd been close, the barkeep had told me. Very close.

The plot, as they say, thickened.

"Great copy, Melanie," I said over our cubicle divider.

Weary-eyed, Melanie peered back at me through her thick, auburn hair.

"Thanks, Sean," she said. "Were you able to use much of it?"

"I'm leading with the Mom, if that helps," I told her.

She grinned. "Yeah, that bit about the photo of him playing lacrosse was pretty good, wasn't it?"

"It was perfect," I said. "Now, go on, get out of here. I'll see you in the morning."

I watched as Melanie shoved some stuff into a forest-green, L.L. Bean backpack that was slung over the back of her chair.

"Good night, Sean."

"'Night, Melanie," I said, watching her leave.

By nine-thirty, I was home, munching a club sandwich. And at ten, I was watching the Yankees lose a meaningless mid-season game to the Anaheim Angels.

I washed down a bite of sandwich with a sip of La Batt Blue as Aaron Judge grounded out in the eighth.

A look of disgust crossed Judge's face as the cameraman closed in for a tight shot while the Yankee strode angrily back to the dugout.

"I know how you feel, pal," I said, toasting the screen with my beer.

Somewhere around eleven o'clock, I fell into a deep, dream-less sleep.

When I woke, the sun was streaming through my living room window, burning into my eyes, and reminding me that I'd fallen asleep in my clothes yet again.

By Sean Flynn, Michael Vivian, and Melanie Goslin Banner Staff Writers

ELIZABETHTOWN -- _Peter Andre's mother keeps a framed photograph of her son, smiling in his lacrosse uniform, on top of the television at her home on Cobble Lane here.

"He was always so focused," Margaret LaGault-Andre, said of her son, who has been identified by police as the driver in a fatal accident on Cameron Street in Harrisburg on Tuesday night. "Whatever it was, he put 100 percent into it. He was a winner."

Harrisburg City Police told The Banner that Andre, 26, of the 2300 block of North Front Street, had traces of cocaine in his system and a blood-alcohol level of almost twice the legal limit when his 2014 Honda Accord plowed into a utility pole across the street from the Cameron Street Brewing Co.

There were no witnesses to the crash that claimed the life of Andre, the chief-of-staff to state Sen. J. Clarence McGeehan, D-Philadelphia, the chairman of the powerful Senate Appropriations Committee.

Adding to the mysterious circumstances surrounding Andre's death, police said the young legislative aide had been shot in the side once with a small caliber weapon, most likely a .22 handgun. It is still not known whether Andre was traveling alone or with a passenger in the fatal crash.

Witnesses, who spoke on condition of anonymity, said Andre had been seen arguing with a woman on the night he died. Police declined to comment.

Conversations with Andre's family and friends painted a picture of an extraordinarily driven young man who was considered an up-and-comer in Democratic circles.

McGeehan declined a request for an interview. His office released a statement calling Andre a "trusted aide and dear friend," who would be "sorely missed by all who knew him."

Veteran Harrisburg lobbyist and union leader Rocco Giambone, who worked with Andre on grants that led to the redevelopment of vast swaths of McGeehan's Philadelphia district, called the young aide "one of the smartest kids I'd ever seen."

"He was just that sort of guy, the one who you knew was going places," Giambone said yesterday.

Tenants at Andre's apartment complex, River House, described him as a friendly neighbor who had helped organize the complex's annual Christmas party.

"He was just the kind of tenant you'd like to have," River House leasing manager Frances Cloud told The Banner yesterday.

Andre was born on June 5, 1992 and educated at local schools. He graduated from Penn State in 2010, where he was president of the college chapter of the Young Democrats and obtained a degree in political science.

While still, an undergraduate, Andre volunteered for the reelection campaign of House Democratic Whip Howard Klein of Elk County. Andre has been credited with helping to keep the seat Democratic in an area of the state where Republicans enjoy a more than 2-1 registration margin, said state Democratic Chairman Donald Rangel.

"He had one of the sharpest eyes for detail and organization that I'd ever seen in someone his age," Rangel said. "He was definitely going somewhere."

He joined McGeehan's staff in 2015, rising quickly to become the top aide to the Philadelphia powerhouse.

Andre was engaged to his high school and college sweetheart, Melissa Fitzgerald, 23, of Elizabethtown. The pair planned a fall wedding in Hershey.

Sitting on a swing-set where they'd played as children, Fitzgerald wept as she described her planned "fairy-tale wedding" to her fiancé.

"Who would do this to him?" Fitzgerald asked a Banner reporter more than once. "Who would do this to him?"

sean.flynn@bannernews.com (717)885-6628

CHAPTER 7

And then I didn't think about Peter Andre or his murder for a while.

As is so often the case in the news business, the story petered out after three or four days – a task that was made easier by the fact that the cops had yet to find his killer.

I still checked in with Marty Herman once a week to see if anything had broken, but the veteran investigator was busy with other cases and had moved on, as I had, to other things.

As a broiling July gave way to a repressively humid August, Harrisburg's Allison Hill district exploded with a late summer spasms of drug-fueled gun violence.

Those stories kept my hands full for most of that summer, as I ventured up to doorways of rowhouses along Derry Street, and the high-numbered streets where most of white Harrisburg didn't tread if it didn't have to.

The interviews always went the same. A look of contempt from my mostly African-American interview subjects, who wondered why The Banner only ventured into the 'hood when something had gone wrong. Though no one ever said it, it was clear that the survivors of these horrors would have preferred it if a black reporter had been the one posing the questions.

And I couldn't blame them. Their experiences were as far from my own as I could imagine. But it was the kind of reporting that I enjoyed the most.

I spent a lot of weekends in Washington D.C. that summer, as well. The nation's capital was a little more than two hours to the south down Interstate 83. And I lost more than a few Saturday afternoons watching the Washington Nationals try to make a season of it as they languished in the lower reaches of the National League.

I also dated a woman from the advertising department, a fiery Italian named Gina.

We didn't have a lot in common, we soon found out. And without talking about it, the flirtation lapsed, and a regretful silence settled over us as we passed in the halls and the clock ticked down to Labor Day.

Fall arrived the way it always did suddenly, and with an explosion of color from the trees that lined the river walk along Front Street.

The snap in the air became more noticeable, and medium-weight jackets replaced Bermuda shorts and t-shirts. By early October, the Yankees had been put out of playoff contention by an Anaheim Angels team that had been their bane throughout the regular season.

So, it was on a clear, cold morning in mid-November that I arrived at the office to find an overstuffed manila envelope waiting for me.

It was at the bottom of a pile of mail that had accumulated after a four-day weekend in Chicago, where I'd caught up with some old friends and did the kind of things that take longer and longer to recover from when you're on the down-slope to forty and gathering speed.

I threw away most of the mail as I checked voicemail and changed my message to let callers know I'd returned from my brief hiatus.

The envelope was weathered and dirty, but it was absent any postmarks, which meant it had been hand-delivered.

I cast a quizzical glance at Vic Young, the day City Editor, who was striding down the row of cubicles toward his desk.

"Vic," I said leaning back in my chair as I passed. "You see who dropped this off?"

He shook his head, scattering dandruff from his squirrel's nest of a comb-over.

"Nope. Probably was dropped off at the front desk and the couriered up here by one of the news assistants," he said, stalking off in the direction of a fire department scanner that had crackled noisily to life.

I inspected the envelope. The label addressing it to "Sean Flynn, The Harrisburg Banner," had been printed on an ink-jet printer.

The sender had neatly trimmed the excess paper and taped the label to the front of the envelope, robbing me of the chance to guess at gender.

The clasp and seal had been taped over with heavy mailing tape that strained to hold a cargo of what felt like a heavy sheaf of documents. I grabbed a pair of scissors from a desk drawer, ran the blade along the taped seal and carefully tore the envelope open at the top.

I pulled out a thick pile of documents held together with a large crocodile clip. Affixed to the top was a greeting card-sized envelope addressed to me in a looping, female hand.

The card was plain white and without any decoration. Inside, the same careful hand had written: *"The answer is there. Someone killed Peter Andre. Follow the money."*

My eyebrows arched in surprise. And I read the note over again before turning my attention to the documents: more than 100 pages of campaign finance reports for a political action committee called the Better Government Association of Pennsylvania.

The group listed offices in Chester County, and a guy named Rocco Giambone was the treasurer.

Flipping to the back of the thick pile of reports, I found the earliest dated back five years ago.

The most recent came from the election season that had concluded the previous autumn. I glanced through some of the donor names, recognizing a few significant ones from central Pennsylvania. But most I did not.

It took another forty minutes to get through that initial inspection.

When I was done, I was left with a picture of a group that attracted donors from the right and the left, as well as from business and organized labor. But I needed to know more and that was going to take time.

Further, I needed to know about the donors. And that meant, as much as it pained me, that I needed help from Mike Vivian.

I glanced down the row of desks, and found him, four down, and kitty-cornered, with a phone resting against his right ear, as he nodded and took notes.

I picked up the sheath, took a deep breath, and walked down the narrow aisle to where Vivian was sitting.

CHAPTER 8

"We're going to' be here all night, Flynn," Mike Vivian wheezed as he inspected the campaign finance reports that covered the long and low conference table.

"You got something better to do tonight, Mike?" I asked him, as I thumbed a sheaf of documents nearest to me. We were in a conference room just off The Banner's main newsroom.

Track lighting cast friendly shadows on the wall, and, outside, the lights of Harrisburg flickered peacefully in the early fall evening. The room was teak-paneled and framed black-and-white prints of important scenes in Harrisburg's history were spaced about five inches apart on all four walls.

"Matter of fact, I do," Vivian said, casting me with a baleful glance. "My kid's got a soccer game. My wife's working late. And I got a story about the new sports book in Philly that I gotta' finish."

I collapsed into an oversized leather conference chair with a high back and padded armrests. I closed my eyes and rubbed my temples wearily.

"Fine," I said, without opening my eyes. "Go on and go. I had the mistaken impression that you might want in on this."

"There are more than four-hundred pages of documents here, Sean," Vivian said. He'd crossed to the other side of the table and was looking over the piles of photocopied reports that had been separated out by year and then by campaign cycle. The reports covered the table from end-to-end in a blanket of cumbersome state bureaucracy.

"Mike," I said.

"What?"

"Just do me one favor: Take a look at the most recent cycle of reports and tell me if any names jump out at you."

Vivian sighed in exasperation and slumped into a chair just across the table from me. The low light played off the planes of his face, casting shadows over his gaunt cheekbones as his limp blonde hair hung into his eyes.

He looked up just a moment later.

"Here's one thing you need to know," he said.

"What's that?"

"Rocco Giambone, the treasurer?"

"Yeah? We quoted him in our story, remember?" I said.

Vivian nodded in assent.

"I remember," he said. "He's a big Democratic money man from Chester County. Used to be an organizer for the carpenters' union in Philly. Now, I think, he runs some kind of consulting business. He's got offices here in town, on State Street."

That meant Giambone had installed himself on Lobbyist Row, a block of rehabbed row houses and historic buildings just across Third Street from the long steps that led to the Capitol's main entrance. It was a prestigious address.

"Giambone ever have any of the usual organized labor problems?" I asked.

"You mean, 'Was he ever indicted?'" Vivian retorted, without looking up from the report he was inspecting.

"Un-hunh."

"He was indicted twice. Both times on tax fraud charges. The U.S. Attorney in Philly was never able to make it stick, though. Drove him crazy. I ran into Giambone on the courthouse steps after the indictments were quashed. He was grinning like the cat who had all the cream."

"You would be, too," I said.

"Yep," Vivian said, and then he was quiet again as he flipped through pages.

"Usual mix of Republican and Democratic donors," he said. "Makes sense. They're covering their bets. Never can tell which side is gonna' win. Might as well make nice with both of 'em."

He stood up and stretched.

"That's about all I see right now," he said, throwing his narrow shoulders back and stretching his long, skinny arms well above his head. "I really gotta' go, Sean."

I waved him off.

"Go ahead," I said. "I'm gonna' stay and work on this a little longer. Thanks for your help, Mike."

"You're welcome, Sean," Vivian said, leaving the conference room door ajar as he exited into the noisy newsroom.

It was just after six o'clock – dinnertime. I wandered back through the Banner newsroom, exchanging greetings with a few colleagues, as I made my way to a staircase that led down what The Banner's management liked to refer to as a cafeteria.

In reality, it was a bank of vending machines that along with the usual chips, candy and soda dispensers, also included one machine that vomited forth microwaveable burgers and ready-to-eat sandwiches.

I selected a ham-and-Swiss, a 20-ounce bottle of Diet Coke, and a bag of locally made potato chips and headed back upstairs.

As I passed my desk, I grabbed a legal pad and a fresh pen to replace the one I'd chewed down to the nub during my interlude with Vivian. It was a nervous habit I'd acquired during my early years of covering endless planning-and-zoning meetings.

Three hours later, I didn't know much more than I had when I started off.

But, on the upside, I did have a legal pad that was scrawled with names, addresses, employment information and donation amounts that I'd later have to enter into a spreadsheet program so that I could cross-reference them and fool around with the data to my heart's content.

Usually, that kind of work was the province of investigative writers.

But a few years back, I'd taken a course on computer-assisted reporting at the Pennsylvania Newspaper Association's stately headquarters at the far, northern end of Front Street. I'd enjoyed my afternoon of fiddling with spreadsheets and databases so thoroughly that I now took any excuse I could to mess around with piles of unsorted data.

One such excursion, based on a Freedom-of-Information request, had led to my exposing massive overtime charges within the police department.

Marty Herman still hadn't forgiven me for that one.

He'd used the overtime to buy a pontoon boat that he sailed on the Susquehanna in the summertime. I'd christened it the S.S. Taxpayer. I didn't get invited on it very much.

Just before ten o'clock, I gathered up the torrent of reports and clipped each year together carefully before I put them back inside the manila envelope in which they arrived.

I turned off the lights and closed the door, blinking against the fluorescent harshness of the newsroom outside.

Melanie Goslin and Brent Vernet were still at work when I arrived at my desk. I locked the reports in a top drawer and grabbed my satchel.

"You two gonna' be done anytime soon?" I asked.

Melanie and Vernet looked up from their computers like startled moles, their faces a sickly white in the reflected light of their monitors.

"Huh?" Melanie asked wearily.

"I said, 'Are you going to be finished any time soon," I enunciated each word carefully. "Drinks? The Oasis? Who's in?

Vernet shook his head.

"Gotta' finish this story and then get home," he said. "I was out after work earlier this week. I do it again, and my wife'll leave me."

I smiled a smile of pity at my married colleague.

"Price you pay for domestic bliss," I said. "What about you, Goslin?" I jerked my head in Melanie's direction.

She gazed back sadly.

"I can't either," she said. "Tomorrow's Friday, and I'm catching an early train to Pittsburgh to visit my sister and her kids."

I glared at both of them.

"Whatever happened to the good, old days when reporters would stay out all night, drink themselves blind and then get up early the next morning to chase a story? Mike Royko would be appalled at you two."

Melanie grinned wickedly, and shot back, "Sean, you're the only one of the three of us who's old enough to remember that kind of stuff."

She cackled as I deflated.

"You two are evil," I said, as I retreated. "You're going to come back in the next life as slugs. I'm outta' here."

Goslin and Vernet laughed and exchanged high-fives, while I beat as dignified a retreat as my 39-year-old body would allow.

In the parking lot, I waited as the phone synced with my car.

A few seconds later, the debut disc from The Libertines began to play. The young Englishmen blasted their Clash-inspired punk rock as I nosed my ten-year-old car out of the parking lot and onto the deserted street.

One left- and two right-turns later, I pulled onto Second Street's restaurant row. It was jumping for a school night in November, and gaggles of twenty-somethings made their way down the street, ducking under brightly lit awnings into the dark clubs that awaited them. Bass-heavy music thumped out of the doorways as they entered.

I drove north further down Second, keeping the river and Front Street off my left shoulder, to where it crossed Pine Street. I found a parking spot between two Vespa scooters and a tricked-out Dodge Neon.

Three minutes later, I was across Second Street and opening the heavy wood door that led into The Oasis.

Someone shouted my name as I entered.

CHAPTER 9

The Oasis had been a couple of things before it was a bar. It was a furniture store. It was a restaurant. And then it was an art gallery. For a long time, it wasn't much of anything at all. But, then, two years ago, a pair of lobbyists looking for a way to shelter their money bought the space, gutted it, and replaced it with what they probably imagined was a taste of Ye Olde London in Harrisburg.

Dark wood abounded. The bar had been imported from some family-owned pub in Yorkshire that had allegedly served beer to King Arthur – or at least that's what the menu, a canny mix of English favorites and American bar grub repurposed with old country-style names – claimed.

I liked The Oasis because the bartender, a gregarious, transplanted New Yorker named Tom McDermott, mixed the best drinks in town. The Oasis also had one of the hippest jukeboxes in the city.

It was stocked with a mix of punk and garage rock classics. As I entered, The Seeds' "Pushin' Too Hard" blared from the speakers mounted on each wall.

Teddy Tigue, a political consultant I knew, was standing at the bar as I entered. Though it was long past office hours, Tigue was still in his work clothes and looked as meticulously put together as he probably had when he had left the house that morning.

He wore a dark suit of Italian cut, an immaculately starched white shirt, and a thin, dark tie with a flawless knot and perfect dimple.

His top button was undone -- his only concession to the lateness of the hour. His brown hair was cut close to his scalp, and a pair of rimless glasses framed the lines of his face. Tigue was obsessive about working out, and his clothes fit him well.

His was the voice that greeted me as I walked in from the street.

As was often the case, Tigue was flanked by two women who stood on either side of him at the bar.

The woman on Tigue's right shoulder was a brunette with a happy, dark Irish face, and ring of freckles on the bridge of her nose.

Her eyes sparkled in the low light, and she threw back her head and laughed with gusto at whatever tired line Tigue had just fed her. She wore a dark turtleneck tucked into a pair of jeans that were matched by a pair of dark boots. The boots gleamed with polish.

Her companion, on Tigue's left, and nearest to me as I entered, was a strawberry blonde who was the light-colored yin to her friend's dark yang.

Her hair, which shone brightly in the light, was slicked back against her head with some sort of shiny substance, and tied into a ponytail that reached the middle of her back.

The result should have been stark and severe. But, instead, it cast her fine-boned features into sharp relief.

She had thoughtful green eyes, and an easy smile that she directed generally at me as Tigue called my name.

She wore a cream-colored sweater matched by a pair of chocolate brown pants. She had obviously given a great deal of thought to her look.

"Sean!" Tigue exclaimed, extending his hand in my direction as I approached. "How are you? Great to see you."

We shook hands. A veteran consultant who had won more campaigns than I cared to count, Tigue was practiced in the arts of making people feel at ease. And he could turn it on and off like a light.

With us, however, the friendship was genuine.

Three years ago, I had helped him through a particularly nasty divorce that had left him almost broke and seen his ex-wife decamp to California with their three-year-old son, a tow-headed blonde named Rudy, whom Tigue loved completely.

"I'm good, Teddy," I said, glancing up appreciatively as Tom, the bartender, slid a South Side cocktail onto the coaster in front of me.

The Seeds gave way to Eddie and the Hot Rods' "Do Anything You Wanna' Do."

Tigue and I chatted genially about the weather, the Yankees' ignominious and early exit from the AL playoffs, and Premier League soccer.

Tigue had played Division Three soccer as an under- graduate, and, through him, I had picked up an appreciation for The Beautiful Game.

On the Saturday mornings when I could manage to wake up early enough, I joined him at the Oasis for a full English breakfast and English League games on television.

"Teddy," I said, taking a sip of my drink and feeling the bracing mix of vodka and lemon juice hit the back of my throat. "Aren't you going to introduce me to your friends?"

Tigue raised his hands in a gesture of mock surrender.

"Sean, I'm sorry," he replied. "I just don't know where my manners have gone. Forgive me." He smiled sarcastically, and I ignored it.

Tigue put a hand on the brunette's shoulder, and said, "This is Heather. She works for Totten, Weinberg. You know -- the big firm with offices in Strawberry Square, across from the Capitol?"

I nodded. Heather smiled and extended her hand.

"Sean Flynn," I said. "I work for The Banner."

We shook hands.

"Oh sure," Heather said, smiling. "I recognize your name."

"Nice to meet you," I said.

"You too," Heather said, returning to her drink.

Tigue turned to the strawberry blonde, who, until now, had regarded me silently from behind her drink.

"And this is ..."

"Lena Bergstrom," she said, cutting off Tigue and extending her hand in such a way that it almost looked like she expected me to kiss it.

I was so shocked at the boldness of the gesture that I almost did.

"Sean Flynn," I said, taking her hand, and resisting the urge. "Nice to meet you."

"And you, Mr. Flynn," Lena said, looking me over coolly like I was a car or a horse she was considering whether to purchase.

"Are you going to check my teeth?" I asked, catching her in the gesture.

"I might – later," she said as she turned away from me and ordered another drink.

Ten minutes later, Tigue, Heather, Lena and I were ensconced at a high four-seater kitty-cornered to the Oasis' front door.

The women sat across from us, perching themselves on the high-backed chairs that ringed the table. They ignored us as they gossiped about some woman they both knew.

I jerked my head in Heather's direction.

Tigue smiled and shrugged.

By then, the jukebox had cycled through Eddie and The Hot Rods to a track by The Damned. Motorhead's crushing "Ace of Spades" pounded our ears forty feet into our heads. At the far side of the room, behind the four-sided bar, a local band was setting up its equipment.

It was nearing eleven o'clock.

Getting down to business, I said, "Teddy, I need some information."

Tigue nodded and contemplated his nearly empty drink, a short glass of Jack and Coke. He swallowed some ice cubes and crunched on them.

"I was wondering when you were going to get around to that," he said. "My name doesn't come into it, 'hear?"

"Of course."

He nodded and signaled our waitress for a refill.

"Then, shoot."

"What can you tell me about an outfit that calls itself The Better Government Association of Pennsylvania?"

"Rocco Giambone's group?"

"Yeah."

"First, I can tell you that they're not much interested in better government. They're just interested in a government that's more responsive to their needs."

"And that makes them different from every other PAC in town how, exactly?" I asked.

Tigue laughed, but it was empty laughter.

"Fair enough," he said, watching as Lena and Heather excused themselves to go to the ladies' room. "But Sean, even you're not so cynical as to believe that those of who are in this game aren't at least partially in it to make the state a better place."

"I'm pretty damn cynical," I said.

"I know you are. And that's what makes you good at what you do. But you also know I'm right."

He looked at me for confirmation. I gave it to him. And he continued.

"But Giambone's in it strictly for the power. You know he's loaded, right? He doesn't have to do it out of a sense of civic-mindedness. He does it because it's a fucking game to him. And he spreads his money around to the horses that he thinks are going to win and that he can control."

Tigue stopped and then looked at me as a server put fresh drinks down in front of both of us.

"Why do you want to know all this?"

I smiled silently and shrugged.

"All right, all right," Tigue asked. "I should know better than to ask. But Seanny, I tell you one thing, if you're looking into something where Giambone is involved, it isn't going to be pretty."

"Thank you," I said.

"You're welcome. And watch your ass," Tigue said. "I don't want to have to go looking for another soccer partner."

Heather and Lena returned from the restrooms.

Twenty minutes later, the four of us were in the front row at the stage as the local band pounded out an energized set of surf rock.

We were pogoing up and down like teenagers as the keyboard player battered his Vox organ and the guitarist bent the strings on the vintage Mosrite he was playing.

The guitarist closed his eyes and gritted his teeth against his bandmates' storm and coaxed wild animal noises from his guitar.

Lena was to my immediate right. Then Heather. And then Tigue. I noticed that the two of them were holding hands and occasionally kissing between numbers.

Between sets, Lena and I staggered to a table, fanning ourselves with bar napkins.

Tigue and Heather had already disappeared. The audience's collective sweat had caused The Oasis' front windows to fog, and the air was thick with the smell of spilled beer.

A waitress passed by and I ordered two glasses of ice water and a pair of Molsons to chase them with. Across from me, Lena smiled broadly and leaned across the table.

"These guys are really good," she said. "They sort of remind me of early Elvis Costello – but with a bit of The Ventures thrown in."

I looked up in surprise.

"Someone knows their pop history," I said, appreciatively. "I was a college dee-jay at Northwestern," Lena said. "It got me into all kinds of different music. My friends at I used to practically live at the Metro."

"Impressive."

Our waitress returned with our drinks and set them in front of us. Around us, the room hummed, and House music thumped from the speakers.

I took a greedy sip of the beer. Lena sipped from the ice water and then followed it with a slug from the amber bottle next to it.

"Northwestern," I said. "That explains the accent."

"Accent?" Lena said quizzically.

"Caught it almost immediately," I said. "I used to work at The Chicago New Times a few years back. Dated a lady from Minnesota. You've got those broad and flat syllables of the upper Midwest. Makes you sound Swedish."

Lena was clearly impressed.

"Nice one, Mr. Flynn," she said, grinning broadly. "I grew up in the Iron Range, along Lake Superior. I guess I don't even hear it anymore."

"Most people wouldn't know unless they had spent any time living out there," I said. "You miss it?"

"I miss my family," she said with a shrug. "But, mostly, it was an excellent place to leave."

"Most places are," I said. We touched glasses. "What do you do, Lena?"

"I work in communications for legislative Democrats. You said you worked for The Banner?" she asked. "You're the guy who wrote about Pete Andre, aren't you?"

I nodded.

"Is there anything new? He was a good friend," she said.

"Nothing new," I told her. It wasn't exactly a lie. But I didn't know her well enough to tell her the truth yet either.

By the end of the night, we were both pleasantly toasted and dancing close together as the band ran through its version of R.E.M.'s "Perfect Circle," from their debut LP, "Murmur."

That record was, for my money, still their finest moment on vinyl.

"You're nice, Sean," Lena murmured into my neck, nuzzling it. "I like you."

"You're not so bad either," I said, returning the compliment.

She lifted her head and broke away from me. Her lips parted, and then we were kissing.

We were still kissing a half-hour later as I fumbled for the light switch in my entryway. We staggered into my living-room and fell onto the couch as my cat screeched its disapproval and jumped out of the way.

There were noises. Then more fumbling. And finally, there were the rhythms of two bodies moving together.

I felt Lena's fingernails dig into my shoulders as she made humming noises into my ear.

When it was over, we kissed like teenagers and slept holding each other on the couch.

CHAPTER 10

Just after lunchtime the next day, I was feeling like a proud papa and grinning goofily at the tidy rows of names, addresses, occupations, phone numbers, and contribution and expenditure amounts that flickered merrily on my computer monitor.

I'd scanned the last five years of the Better Government Association's campaign finance records into my laptop.

It had taken two hours to align the data into neat rows on a spreadsheet program, and then another hour or so to catch glitches and make corrections.

People like to think journalism is like they see it in the movies.

They think reporters spend all their time chasing crime suspects out of courthouses, shoving tape recorders in their faces and asking, "Tommy, why'd you do it?"

Either that, they think we're standing in damp parking garages talking to Hal Holbrook's shadowy outline and palling around with a partner who looks like Dustin Hoffman.

To be fair, I did spend five hours standing in an underground parking garage in Baltimore once. But that was only because I was drunk and had dropped my keys.

The truth, unfortunately, is a lot less glamorous. Really good journalism means spending a lot of time sitting by the phone and waiting for someone to call you back.

It also means a lot of time pawing through municipal records and police reports; sitting through endless public meetings; having doors slammed in your face and getting called names you've never even heard of.

And sometimes it means getting up at six in the morning, leaving behind a beautiful woman and fighting your way through a monster hangover so you can spend an otherwise gorgeous late fall morning tediously inputting numbers into an Apple laptop that's three years out of date. And that's what I'd been doing.

I'd kissed Lena good-bye on my front stoop and watched as she walked briskly up my street.

She'd rejected my offer of a ride back to her place in Midtown.

"It's beautiful out," she said, her head on my shoulder and her pretty mouth very close to my ear. "I'll walk."

Her hair smelled of my shampoo and vaguely like the aftershave I was wearing. A light wind, promising a day full of crisp potential, blew in from the river, which was just across the street from my apartment, and it whipped her lovely strawberry blonde hair around my head.

"I'll call you," I told her as I untangled myself and then watched her walk away.

"I know you will," she said. And then I watched her until she was out of sight.

So here I was wrestling five years' worth of campaign finance records into shape. I'd gotten odd stares when I traipsed into the office that morning, smiling to myself, and humming the "Peter Gunn" theme by Henry Mancini.

"What are you doing here?" Vic Young, the day city editor said, without looking up from that morning's edition of The Banner.

"Got some work to do," I said. "Thought I'd get a head-start."

"Your shift doesn't start until four," he said, still not looking up.

"So, shoot me for being ambitious."

He cast a quizzical glance and walked away.

After lunch, I tapped some keys and thought a little bit about what I knew so far.

Peter Andre was still dead. That hadn't changed, which was reassuring because I'd never had to cover a resurrection before.

I had five years' worth of campaign finance reports for a political action committee run by a guy who may or may not have – or had – ties to some unsavory characters.

The dead guy worked for one of the most powerful state legislators in Pennsylvania. The state legislator was from Philadelphia. The guy who ran the PAC was from suburban Philly.

Where was the connection?

I tapped some more keys and played with the data a bit more.

My eyes widened correspondingly.

I had something … maybe.

"Vic, I called. "Would you come over here and look at something for a minute?"

"What Flynn?" he said irritably, as I startled him out of his reverie over a cup of gas station coffee. "I'm busy."

"Just come here," I said. "I want to show you something."

Young rose heavily from his chair and walked wearily down the aisle to my desk.

Around us, The Banner newsroom was just beginning to fill. Most newsrooms don't really get going until ten or eleven in the morning. The staff was known to stretch this informal start time at least twice a week.

"What?" Young said, leaning on my chair and rubbing his eyes,

"Remember that legislative staffer who got shot on Cameron Street over the summer?"

"Yeah, sure," he said. "I remember. They never caught the shooter. Kid's name was Andre or something."

"Right," I said. "He worked for Sen. Clarence McGeehan from Philly."

"Okay."

I directed Young's attention to the expenditure row in the spreadsheet.

"Look who's getting a ton of money," I said, highlighting more than three-dozen entries for McGeehan over the last five years.

"Uh-huh," he said. "Someone's giving McGeehan money. No crime there."

"Right," I said. I reached to my desk and pulled the nearest stack of campaign finance reports into my lap.

"But look who runs the PAC," I said, pointing my finger at a box detailing the Better Government Association's personnel.

"I'll be a sonofabitch," Young said, his eyebrows arching in surprise the way they did when he thought he might have actual news occurring in front of him.

"Exactly," I said.

Thirty minutes later, I was standing outside Rocco Giambone's office on State Street, reading a magazine, and waiting for him to come out.

That's another thing people really don't know about newspaper reporters. We spend a lot of time standing around. When I was younger, and just starting out covering cops, I used to bitch a lot about all the standing around I had to do.

To my untrained eyes, all those years ago, it felt like the news should just be delivered to us on a silver platter.

That all changed when I was out on a stake-out with an older reporter on the staff of another newspaper on a freezing day in the middle of January.

We were standing on the edge of the woods at a state forest and the snow was nearly up to the tops of our boots. A harsh, cold wind whipped the side of the mountain where the plane, a Cessna, had gone down.

One by one, the TV and radio reporters started to melt away. And, after around six hours, I was about ready to do the same.

"Forget this, I'm getting out of here," I told the older reporter as I watched the news crews pile into their warm vans and drive away.

The old veteran from the competing newspaper smiled ruefully at me.

"I wouldn't do that if I were you, kid," he said.

"Why? It's freezing. We're not going to learn anything here that we can't follow by phone."

"Just wait," the old vet said.

Ten minutes later, the investigators emerged from the woods. One of the leaders motioned to me and the older reporter. He took us back into the woods, to the crash site, where the twisted wreck of the plane had slammed, nose-first, into the side of a cliff. A small group of people stood around the wreckage.

"Who're they?" I asked the lead investigators.

"Families of the deceased," the lead investigator said. "We choppered them in so they could see the wreck first hand. And they want to talk."

I looked at the old vet from the other newspaper.

"I told you to wait," he said, with a wry grin.

I was glad I did. He and I were the only two reporters to get the interviews with the crash victims' families

I never forgot that lesson.

I was prepared to wait for Rocco Giambone for as long as it took. It was damp and cold, but at least it wasn't raining.

And I had a new pen.

CHAPTER 11

Rocco Giambone's office was in a tidy brick rowhouse about two-thirds of the way down State Street near its intersection with Second Street.

Looking down State from the Capitol end, I could see more of the rowhouses that made up Lobbyist's Row before it collided with Front Street and then Kunkel Plaza, and Riverfront Park beyond that.

Behind me, on the other side of Third Street, the impressive stone edifice of the state Capitol loomed on its high hill.

Built in 1906, funded by robber baron money, and dedicated (a touch ironically, I always thought) by Theodore Roosevelt, the building's denizens had never really lost the sense of entitlement or privilege bestowed on them by the wise grey hairs so many years before.

In Pennsylvania, the state government is all-encompassing. There are few areas of public life it doesn't touch.

Need to get your kid into Penn State? Call your local legislator. Having a problem getting a pothole fixed? Chances are if you knew someone in the right place, you could get it paved in a jiffy.

Got money to burn and a building you needed built? You had a sympathetic ear on the Hill – as long as you knew you'd have to return the favor with a do-nothing job for someone's idiot cousin.

The building's gold dome glinted imperiously in the sun as if reminding us, "I have always been here. I will always be here. You will always need me."

A damp wind blew in from the river, piercing my overcoat and settling on my bones like an unwelcome houseguest.

I pulled my scarf – a red tartan number -- a little more tightly about my throat, opened the door to Giambone's building and mounted a narrow set of stairs that led to his office on the second floor.

If you didn't know what to look for, Giambone's office would have been easy to miss. When I reached the top of the landing, I came face-to-face with a whitewashed door with a little gold nameplate screwed into the center of it with two, gold Philips head screws.

"Better Government Association of Pennsylvania," it announced unceremoniously. I turned the matching gold knob. It wiggled in my hand but did not allow me entry. I put an ear to the door. Through the plywood of the door, I could hear muffled conversation and the insistent ring of a telephone.

Lacking any other options, I knocked. Twice.

And then I waited. Somewhere behind the door, there was movement. I heard heavy footfalls, and then the door opened.

The face that stared back at me was not a friendly one.

"Can I help you?" the older man at the door asked.

In my frame of vision, there was a steel desk that looked like it had been pilfered from a middle school garage sale, two folding chairs, a side table whose veneer had been chipped away on one corner, exposing the particle board beneath, and the edge of a gray filing cabinet.

It did not look like the sort of office that belonged on Lobbyist Row.

In fact, it looked barely used at all.

I must have been staring, because the man, already impatient, repeated, "Can I help you?"

His tone, if it was possible, was even less friendly.

I handed him a business card. I had always liked the Banner's cards.

They were printed on heavy stock with optimistic raised lettering in an old-fashioned newspaper typeface.

The paper's slogan proclaimed, in schoolboy Latin "*Scientia Est Potentia*" – "Knowledge is Power."

The man regarded my business card. He did not look impressed. In fact, he looked like she might shove it up my nose.

"Sean Flynn from The Banner to see Mr. Giambone," I said.

"He's busy," the man said.

"I just need him for five minutes," I said hopefully. "It won't take long at all."

"He's busy," the man said again, more insistently this time, as he began to close the door. "Call for an appointment."

"Two minutes!" I yelped as the door closed.

"Is that your final answer?" I said to the empty hallway.

The door, still white with the Better Government Association's nameplate screwed into the center of it, did not answer.

"So, I'll wait," I mumbled to myself as I trudged back down the narrow stairs.

Years ago, someone had nailed a runner to the floorboards in an attempt at sprucing things up.

Now the runner was threadbare. The exposed boards needed a fresh coat of varnish and the stairs sagged as if signaling defeat. I got splinters just looking at the whole arrangement.

Out in the street, I set up station-keeping outside Giambone's office.

A gnarled oak, whose roots had pushed up the sidewalk, and created spiderweb fractures in the paving stones, provided me an excellent place to lean.

But it was still damp, and it was still cold. And I didn't have any coffee.

I stamped my feet to keep warm, retied my scarf and thrust my hands deeper into my pockets as I tried not to look suspicious. It turned out I was worried about nothing.

The growing lunchtime crowd that was streaming down the long marble stairs to the Capitol's front entrance barely paid me any heed as they made a beeline for the restaurants along Second Street.

After 40 minutes of standing the damp cold, Giambone emerged from his office flanked by two guys in their twenties who looked like they ate iron filings for breakfast.

They stared back at me with just the appropriate hint of malice.

Giambone, it could be charitably said, had not seen the inside of a gym for some time.

His wool overcoat was expensive and stretched tight over a prodigious stomach. He wore a Burberry scarf wrapped so tightly around his throat that it pushed at least three of his chins into the bottom of his face.

That, in turn, compressed the rest of his face, leaving his features blurry and indistinct.

Giambone's brown eyes were scrunched close together in his fat face. They were bright and mean and utterly without the hint of knowledge.

But that look was deceptive. You didn't get as far as he did in the cutthroat world of organized labor without being smart. His foes, and there were many, crossed him at their peril.

I approached him, and out of the corner of my eye, I could see the two goons tense up.

"Mr. Giambone," I said as the union boss made a right out of his office and tried to head up State Street toward the Capitol.

He turned to me.

"Whatchoo want?" he said, with a thick South Philadelphia accent.

"Sean Flynn from The Banner," I said. "I'd just like a minute of your time to ask you about your PAC's interest in Senator Clarence McGeehan and what you might know about the death of Peter Andre."

"I don't know what you're talking about," he said. "I got no interest in Clarence McGeehan and I don't know this kid, Peter Whatsisname."

He turned away and resumed his walk toward the Capitol.

"I think you do, Sir," I said as I fell into step behind him, my phone wedged under his nose. "Your PAC gave Senator McGeehan more than $250,000 over the last five years. And Mr. Andre was Senator McGeehan's chief-of-staff until he was killed over the summer."

"We give money to a lot of people," Giambone said. He continued to walk; his face turned forward. He didn't look at me.

The walking, however, wasn't easy. He was breathing heavy by the time he hit the curb. He was wheezing as he made his way up the Capitol steps.

"But not as much as you give to McGeehan," I said. "You've given him more than any other senator. How do you account for that?"

As much as it is possible for someone who weighs 275 pounds to do, Giambone whirled on me and pointed a gloved finger the size of a small sausage into my chest.

His breath, at close range, smelled of coffee and cigarettes.

"Listen, you pipsqueak," he said. "I got nothing to say to you. Now fucking beat it before you write your own obituary."

"These seem like reasonable questions, Mr. Giambone," I said, swallowing back a knot of fear in my throat. "I just want to know how your PAC spends its money. You're influencing campaigns. Don't you think the public has a right to know?"

Giambone shoved me and nodded to his two bruisers.

"You don't have a right to know a thing," he said, pushing me back. "Tino, Eddie, explain to him that I don't gotta explain myself."

The one called Tino – his hair was a slightly brighter shade of blonde than his twin, and his eyes were green to the other's blue – approached me.

"You heard him. Get lost," he said, giving me a hard shove in the shoulders. I stumbled backward on the stairs but was proud of myself for keeping my balance.

"All right. All right," I said to the two bruisers. "I'm leaving. I get the point."

I watched Giambone get smaller as he went further up the stairs. The two bruisers, each wearing matching black satin warm-up jackets and ironed blue jeans, followed him into the building through its main entrance.

I grinned as I watched Giambone leave.

The story the next morning was on the Banner's front page. It was under my byline.

The headline read, *"Labor Boss Menaces Reporter: Giambone Won't Answer Questions About PAC."*

That was when things got really bad.

CHAPTER 12

Two nights later, Lena and I were walking the backstretch of Riverfront Park near my apartment. We'd picked up the trail that ran parallel to the Susquehanna River across the street from the courthouse on Market Street and headed south toward my house in Shipoke.

"I have quite a night planned for you," I told her, as she rested her head against my shoulder in the gathering darkness of a work night. "You'll be so happy that you won't want to go home."

Lena gave me a quick peck on the cheek.

"Why Mr. Flynn, whatever did you have in mind?" she asked sleepily. She'd bagged out early from work and met me at The Banner's offices on Market Street, just a few blocks from the Capitol complex.

"Guy I know runs a restaurant, taught me how to make Veal piccata the other night. Paired it with this unbelievable wine from New Zealand. And I've got an apple pie from Bernstein's Bakery on Third that you're going to love."

"Sounds wonderful," she said, smiling in the chilly evening. "Can I have vanilla ice cream with my apple pie? And will you warm it up for me?"

I stopped dead in my tracks, a look of mock horror crossing my face.

"Why Miss Bergstrom," I said, putting my hands on my hips and striking an outraged pose. "I thought you'd been brought up better than that. Everyone knows that you serve a wedge of Vermont cheddar cheese with apple pie."

Lena's lovely blue eyes narrowed, and she poked me emphatically in the chest.

"That might be the way they do it in that snooty, glorified country club of a town where you grew up, Mr. Flynn," she said. "But us simple Midwestern ladies have our apple pie, warm, with vanilla ice cream. And if I don't get my way ... you don't get yours later."

I laughed and raised my hands in surrender.

"Anything for you, my darlin'," I said.

Lena grinned contentedly, took my hand again, and settled her head back onto my shoulder.

"Better believe it," she said.

We were walking under a railroad overpass less than a block from my apartment and were making plans for the weekend when a pair of thick-necked goons emerged from the darkness.

Both had shaved heads and mean eyes.

"You Sean Flynn?" the first thug, dressed in a cable-knit black turtleneck asked me. His biceps were straining against the cloth. And there was a bulge in his right, front pocket that I was pretty sure wasn't his wallet.

I stepped in front of Lena, whose eyes were wide and bright with fear. I puffed out my chest, hoping that would distract them away from the fact that my knees were shaking.

"What's it to you?" I shot back, in what I hoped was my best James Cagney voice.

The second thug, who was wearing a light, ill-fitting warm-up jacket that barely contained a generous gut, stepped forward and jabbed his index finger so hard into my sternum that it pushed me backward, said, "You should be careful what you write about."

He cast an evil glance at Lena, who I felt tighten her grip on my shoulder. Her breathing was quick and shallow.

"Especially since you got such a pretty lady friend," he continued.

I was getting tired of the game.

"I write a lot of stories," I said. "You guys mad at one in particular? Or do you just have a lot of free-floating rage? They got counseling for that now."

"That a joke?" the first thug asked.

"Maybe," I said, trying to put as much of myself between Lena and the goombahs as possible.

"Well, here's another punchline," Thug. No. 1 said as he hit me, hard, in the stomach. I felt the air whoosh out of me, as I doubled over in pain.

There was another blow, this time to the back of my head. And I heard Lena scream. As I went down, I felt someone club me on the ears.

Lena screamed again.

And then I was on the ground, trying to cover myself as I felt heavy boots crash into my ribcage, stomach, and arms. I covered my head with my hands and tried to regain my feet.

But each time I tried, a heavy, slab-like fist collided with my jaw, and I went down again. After the third punch, I stayed down. I felt blood in my mouth, and my face felt swollen and puffy. I would not look glamorous in the morning.

As I lay on the ground on a cold, November night, the second thug leaned down close to my ear.

"Stay the fuck away from the Better Government Association," he said. "Or next time, you're dead."

Then things went cold and small and black. As I fell into the darkness, I heard a siren.

And I thought I felt Lena's hand warm on my cheek. Then I didn't hear anything at all.

When I woke up, I was in a hospital room. The fluorescent light above me was cold and impersonal. The blankets were scratchy.

And as my eyes swam back into focus, I saw Lena, Marty Herman, and the Banner's executive editor, Bernie O'Neill, seated in a half-circle around my bed.

Lena's eyes were worn and tired, and they were red from crying. There was knitting in her lap, and a mass-market paperback was on a bedside table next to me.

O'Neill, a gregarious guy with thick, dark eyebrows and a head of salt and pepper hair that defied his efforts to style it, sat to Lena's left.

His green-and-blue striped Rep tie was loosened, and his blue Oxford was open at the collar.

I felt a stab of pain in my arm and felt the IV needle that fed a cocktail of industrial strength painkillers through a slender length of surgical tubing. The pain ate away at the edges of the pleasant chemical bliss the painkillers delivered.

Marty Herman was in plainclothes. He was wearing a blue tee-shirt, jeans and a pair of scuffed sneakers. His brow was creased, and he chewed on a toothpick.

"I'm here," I said weakly. Lena's eyes brightened, and she leaned forward and grabbed my hand. Then she stood up and kissed me gently on the forehead.

"You're awake," she murmured, her hair falling into my eyes. "I missed you."

"Nice to be missed," I croaked. "How long I been here?"

It was Marty Herman who spoke next.

"Two days," he said. "For some reason, the doctors felt like your life was worth saving."

"I'll have to remember to thank them for that," I said, then looked at Lena. "I heard sirens before I blacked out. You called '911?'

She shook her head.

"No. A minute or so after those two goons worked you over, a couple with a dog came along and saw me cradling you, and sobbing. They called 911. Lucky we were close to Harrisburg Hospital. They brought you over right away."

I nodded weakly, trying to take it all in. Stars danced behind my eyes as I did. My face felt swollen.

"You and me, we're gonna need to talk," Herman said. "But for now, I'm here to look after you and Miss Bergstrom."

"Marty, you picking up overtime for that?" I asked.

He scowled at me. "Always the watchdog," he barked. "I'm doing this as a public service. No charge to the taxpayers of our fine city."

Bernie O'Neill stepped forward.

"We took care of the medical leave paperwork, Sean," he said. "You take as much time as you need to recover. Naturally, we're taking you off the Peter Andre story."

"Bernie, come on," I protested half-heartedly, unable to conjure up the energy for actual rage. "I've done so much work on this."

O'Neill shook his head sternly.

"No way, Sean," he said. "We're not risking having this happen to you again. And it's a police matter now. You can't be the subject of your own story."

"Always the stickler for rules, weren't you, Bernie?" I said. O'Neill smiled without enthusiasm.

"Rest, Sean," he said. "I mean it."

He turned to leave, and then looked at Lena.

"Make sure he rests, would you, Miss Bergstrom?"

Lena folded her arms on her chest and jerked her head at me.

"I'll try," she said. "But he knows his own mind." O'Neill cast another glance at me over his shoulder. "That's what I'm afraid of."

Then he left. And I was in a dreamless, opioid-induced sleep.

CHAPTER 13

Ten days later, and only feeling slightly less the worse for wear, I was back at the office. True, I was only working half-days, and my face still looked like it had been hit by a Mack truck. But I was back, and that was enough for me.

The Banner, to its eternal credit, had made an insane stink about my run-in with the two toughs.

Our Metro columnist had columnized about it.

And I'd done a couple of interviews with the major journal-ism reviews. The radio and television stations had come calling.

And to them, I read a prepared statement that was drawn up by a legion of lawyers dispatched, no doubt, by our corpo-rate paymasters in Chicago.

In response, the Harrisburg cops had ratcheted up patrols along the river in Shipoke.

And two meatheads matching the description of my alleged attackers had been arrested, charged and then promptly bailed as they awaited their court dates.

That was a source of small comfort to me. But not a bunch.

I was extra careful when I drove home. I even dropped a grand on a new home security system. Lena stayed over often. And when she went home, I drove her.

Bernie O'Neill had told Vic Young, the day City Editor, to keep me under wraps. Phone work. Maybe some soft features. Let me ease back into things.

I wasn't buying it for a minute. Nor was I going to let some kid take over as cops' reporter while they nursed me back to health.

I stood in my office chair to stretch and felt dizzy as the blood rushed to my head. Groaning, I steadied myself on the side of my cubicle. Melanie Goslin rushed over from her cubi-cle to steady me.

"You okay, Sean?" she asked solicitously as she helped lower me back into my chair. Her forehead was creased with concern, and her green eyes sparkled behind her glasses.

"I'm fine, Mel," I said. "It only hurts when I breathe."

She smiled and patted me on the shoulder as she walked back to her cubicle.

"That's my boy," she said.

At Lena's urging, I'd started chipping away again at the Better Government Association's campaign finance records. Hitting some keys, I sorted the data alphabetically, by contributor, and waited for patterns to emerge.

Lena had played a key role in my recovery. While I convalesced at home, she knocked off early most days from work, came over and fixed me dinner, and often stayed overnight.

For the first few nights, there wasn't much for her to do except sit there and watch me not feel good.

For the second five days of my recovery, as my strength returned, she did a little less watching, and a little more participating.

She had a quiet strength and a will that was so forceful that sometimes it knocked you back in your seat.

The night before I came back to the office, we were sitting in my living room.

I'd put on Miles Davis' "Kind of Blue" – clichéd, I know, but that doesn't keep it from being one of the great jazz records of all time. We were sitting together on my couch. Rather, Lena was sitting, and I was laying, my head in her lap, as she ran her fingers through my hair.

"Thanks," I told her. "I don't think I could have pulled through this without you."

She smiled and leaned to kiss me.

"Yes, you could have," she said. "But thanks for saying so anyways."

A long moment passed between us. Miles played. Lena stared down at me, her lips half-parted as if there was something she wanted to say.

"What?" I asked.

She shook her head.

"It's nothing," she said. "Nothing at all." "C'mon. Tell me."

"I..." her voice trailed off. "I ... think ... I think ... I think I'm falling in love with you, Sean."

A single tear ran down a porcelain cheek.

I sat up, took her face in both hands, and looked at her. Right then, it felt like my soul had risen to the top of my neck and was doing everything it could to jump out of my body.

"I love you, Lena," I said, and pulled her to me.

I snapped out my reverie as the data finished sorting. There were hundreds of records, and for a long time, there was nothing to look at.

I'd gotten through the "E's" and the "F's," and was about three-quarters of the way through the "G's," when I noticed a pattern emerging.

There were dozens of donations from a group called "The Greater Doylestown Development Cooperation."

Lots of little contributions, $50 or $100, spread out over the five years' worth of records that I had.

Doylestown, the county seat of Bucks County was a wealthy suburb of broad lawns and over- privileged children about a 45-minute drive north of Philadelphia.

Clicking through another set of commands, I put together a subtotal of contributions from the group. Taken together, they amounted to nearly a half-million dollars. That seemed like an awful lot.

Whistling through my teeth, I minimized the spreadsheet window. In the search bar on Chrome, I typed "Greater Doylestown Development Cooperation."

The search returned about 100 or so records, many of them newspaper articles from a Bucks County weekly. They were badly written, and not particularly enlightening.

Oddly, for the computer age, the Greater Doylestown Development Cooperation did not have a Web site.

The newspaper stories did reveal that it was a non-profit outfit, that its executive director was a guy named Larry Keller, and that it had offices on Court Street in Doylestown.

Glancing up from my computer, I called over to Melanie Goslin.

"Hey, Mel? What's that website where you can look up information about non-profit groups?"

A moment later, a Slack message with the URL materialized on my desktop.

"Thanks," I said, and pulled up the page. I typed the non-profit group's name into the search window.

The federal tax filing allowing the Greater Doylestown Development Cooperation to claim its non-profit status flashed up on the screen.

Just like in the newspaper stories, the non-profit had an address of Court Street in Doylestown. There was also a list of its officers.

And just like in the newspaper stories, a guy named Larry Keller was its executive director.

I scanned past some federal mumbo-jumbo to a list of the company's officers.

And right there, at the top of the list, was one of the missing pieces.

Rocco Giambone was the founder and chief executive officer of the Greater Doylestown Development Cooperation.

Toggling back over to Google again, I entered the names "Keller" and "Giambone" into the search window.

There was a lot of chaff, but the seventh entry on the page seemed promising. I clicked on it, and my eyes went wide at the digital photo I found there. I sent the page to the printer and hurried over to fetch it.

I'm no detective, but I'm pretty sure they refer to what I had just found as a "clue." I folded the printed page in half, lengthwise, and tucked it under the calendar that filled most of my desk.

Then I grabbed a state Capitol phone directory, flipped through a few pages, and started to dial.

"Is Senator McGeehan available?" I asked when a pleasant-voiced woman answered the phone.

Five minutes later, I had a 10:30 a.m. appointment the next morning to see J. Clarence McGeehan.

CHAPTER 14

At exactly 10:31 a.m. the next morning, I was sitting in J. Clarence McGeehan's personal office on the third floor on the Senate side of the state Capitol.

McGeehan chaired the Senate Appropriations Committee, which meant his offices were bigger than most, and his staff even more attentive to their boss's wishes.

McGeehan's desk was a big, sprawling oak affair with clawed feet.

Despite his being such an important personage, it was nearly devoid of paper.

The walls were painted a muted blue, and they were dotted with framed certificates, photos of McGeehan with various governors, presidents and other people of significance, and memorabilia accumulated during 30 years of service in state politics.

I took note of one item, a massive stuffed fish that was mounted on a mahogany plaque on a wall on the far side of McGeehan's office.

McGeehan was sitting behind his desk when I came in. His back was to me, as he pounded away on a computer keyboard that was attached to a big, flat-panel display. He hit a key, and the screen went to black.

He turned in his high-backed, brown leather chair and looked at the young woman who had brought me into his office.

"This is Mr. Flynn, Senator," she said, her voice colored with a deference that verged on indentured servitude.

She was young, maybe 25 or 26, and her hair was stiff and blonde. She had deep brown eyes and olive skin, which made me doubt the veracity of her blonde hair.

McGeehan rose from his chair and gestured me toward an oval conference table across from his desk.

"Come in, Mr. Flynn," he said with a politician's practiced ease. "So good to meet you. Is there anything I can get for you? Coffee? Soda?"

I tried to defer, but Flynn didn't listen, He barked at the young woman, "Estella, bring us two coffees. And some cream and sugar."

"Yes, Senator," Estella said, as she backed out of the room. McGeehan probably forbade his staff from turning their back on him.

Probably made them walk three feet behind him in public too.

McGeehan settled into a chair at the high end of the oval table.

I sat in one across from him, the vast expanse of table separating us. He clenched his hands behind his head and leaned back in his chair.

"We'll just have to wait a moment," he said. "Frank Schildner, my new chief-of-staff, will be joining us."

"Of course," I said.

Although he was well on the other side of sixty, McGeehan didn't look old. He had a full head of white hair that was combed straight back from his forehead.

And even though it was the middle of November, he glowed with a tan that looked fresh from the golf course. His nails were manicured and were shiny with some kind of lacquer.

McGeehan was in short-sleeves, wearing a blue Oxford-cloth button-down and a pair of fastidiously creased grey flannel trousers.

His cordovan loafers were immaculate. A red power tie with little white dots on it was tied in a half-Windsor at this throat.

McGeehan's studied look made me self-conscious about my own fingernails, which were ragged and uneven and bitten down to the quick in some places.

It was a nervous habit that I'd tried mightily to quit. I was also wearing a blue button-down, which, I'm guessing, cost less than his.

My khaki trousers were frayed at the cuffs. And I noted a coffee stain on one thigh with some consternation.

I jerked my head in the direction of the stuffed fish.

"You a big saltwater guy, Senator?" I asked.

He nodded enthusiastically.

"Huge," he said. "I've got a place down in Sarasota. It's been in my family for years. I try to get down there two or three times a year. An old law school buddy and I go fish the Gulf for black grouper and some mangrove and yellow-tail snapper.

"Caught that one last year," he continued, getting up to inspect his trophy. He took a handkerchief from his pocket and wiped some dust from the stuffed fish. "A black grouper. Around four feet long. And tough as a sonofabitch to land. You fish much, Mr. Flynn?"

"I fly fish some," I said. "Don't get nearly as often as I'd like." He nodded.

"Hard to find the time, I'm sure, in your line of work," he said and returned to the table. As he sat, he smoothed out his trousers and made sure that none of his bare ankle was exposed as he crossed one leg over another.

Frank Schildner, the chief-of-staff, entered the room at the same time as the secretary bearing coffee.

She laid a pair of bone china mugs on saucers on the table before us and matched them with a little decanter for the cream and a selection of sugar and artificial sweeteners.

"Thank you," I said as she put the cup down in front of me.

"You're welcome," Estella said with an easy smile. She gave me a look out of the corner of her eye that I didn't quite understand.

McGeehan, who took his coffee black, missed the moment that passed between Estella and me.

He was already talking to his aide, Schildner, about some piece of legislation they were working on.

Schildner was tall and balding, and I judged him to be about forty-five.

Like his boss, he was immaculately dressed in a white shirt, red tie and a pair of braces. His trousers were black, and his black lace-ups were spotless. He was wearing a pair of half-glasses that he'd pushed down his nose.

If I didn't know better, I'd say he was trying to intimidate me.

McGeehan put his cup down on the table and folded his hands before him.

"So, Mr. Flynn," he said. "I'm told you want to talk to me about poor Peter Andre."

"That's right," I said, as I poured a splash of cream into my coffee and chased it with a pair of sugar packets.

McGeehan's brow creased as he gave me a look that, for him, passed for solicitous concern.

"Horrible, horrible thing," he said. "Such a bright guy. Had a great future ahead of him. But I'm not sure that I can tell you much more than what I told Mike Vivian."

"Actually, I'm not really here about Peter Andre, Senator," I said, as I took the folded photo from a pocket inside the blue blazer I was wearing. I flattened the paper and turned it so McGeehan could see it."

McGeehan betrayed no emotion as he looked at the picture of a smiling Rocco Giambone, his arm draped around the shoulder of a paunchy middle-aged guy that the photo caption identified as McGeehan's district chief-of-staff, Larry Keller. In the background, Pete Andre scowled at the camera.

"And this is?" McGeehan asked, trying, not entirely successfully, to keep the sarcasm from creeping into his voice.

"Actually," I said, "I was wondering if you could tell me why one of your employees is the executive director of a non-profit that Rocco Giambone runs – a non-profit that contributes to Giambone's PAC, which also happens to contribute heavily to your re-election efforts."

"That's nonsense," McGeehan said, puffing out his chest in mock indignation.

Schildner, McGeehan's pick to replace the late Peter Andre, stared at me, hard, from the other side of the table.

"Exactly what are you implying here, Mr. Flynn," he said.

"Nothing," I said breezily. "It's just that I'm awfully darn confused about why one of your staffers would be running a non-profit that's basically owned by a labor boss of question- able credentials. The same one, I might add, who had his goons kick the stuffing out of me a week or so back when I asked him too many uncomfortable questions."

McGeehan's nostrils flared, and his already tanned face turned a deeper shade of red. The nice guy façade was gone now. And he was behaving like the person he was: a high-powered pol who was used to getting his way and not being questioned.

"You can't prove that, you low-rent, garbage-sniffer," he said. "I won't have you come in here and make baseless accusations against me or my staff."

He got up from the table and walked briskly away. Schildner rose in his seat.

"I think this meeting is over, Mr. Flynn," he said. "And I think you can find your own way out."

A moment later, I was out the door, and passing by Estella's desk.

"Alas, Estella," I said. "This is goodbye."

"Leaving already?" she asked.

"I know," I said. "And we were just getting started."

She smiled and returned to her computer. I spent a long time waiting for the elevator.

CHAPTER 15

That night, I was at home, making myself steak frites in my little walk-in kitchen and trying to figure out what I knew. There were pieces, but not a plot.

As I rubbed, sliced, and dropped slivers of russet potatoes into a cast iron pan on my stove, I remembered that the first thing I knew was that Peter Andre was still dead. And that was unlikely to change anytime soon.

As the oil sputtered and the potatoes began to brown, I also remembered that I knew Peter Andre had worked for Sen. J. Clarence McGeehan, a state senator from Philadelphia, whose aging preppy front just about concealed the South Philly street tough beneath.

I also knew that McGeehan had a relationship with Rocco Giambone, a union heavy who had his own PAC and donated heavily to McGeehan's campaign.

When the potatoes were done, I put them on a paper towel-covered plate to drain.

I dropped half a New York strip steak that had been seasoned with freshly ground black pepper and kosher salt onto the pan.

I turned the heat on the stove to high and seared each side of the steak for two minutes, before letting it cook for seven minutes on each side to reach a decent medium-rare to medium.

On the stereo in the living room, beneath a framed print for the Jimmy Cliff movie, "The Harder They Come," Disc Two of the 25th-anniversary edition of The Clash's "London Calling" blared from a pair of speakers situated at either end of a pair of bookshelves.

The second disc of the English punk combo's legendary 1979 LP was a collection of demos, rarities, and outtakes that had been presumed lost for years.

The assortment of demos and band chatter was nick-named "The Vanilla Tapes," after the London studio where they were recorded.

According to Clash mythology, the band's longtime roadie Johnny Green was charged with delivering the tapes to "London Calling" producer Guy Stevens. But Green fell asleep on London's tube while on his way to meet the producer.

Waking in a panic at the station where he was to disembark, Green left the tapes on the train as he rushed out.

The "Vanilla Tapes" demos were then consigned to the rubbish bin of history until former Clash guitarist Mick Jones discovered them when he was moving some boxes.

I'd always loved the tapes because they offered an early look into the making of "London Calling," which remains one of my favorite records of all time.

I admit, it's a bit on the Trainspotterish side, but I loved hearing the way the rough cuts were worked into the finished songs.

And really, isn't that what reporters do? We take the rough matter of history and polish it into something that can be consumed by the public.

If only half the stuff I wrote was as much fun to read as "Train in Vain," was to listen to.

The steak was almost done when I resumed my mental catalog of stuff, I knew about Peter Andre's death.

I also knew, for instance, that lobbyist Rocco Giambone ran a non-profit in suburban Bucks County that helped fund his PAC. I also knew that McGeehan's district director was pulling double-duty as executive director of Giambone's non-profit.

By now, the steak had developed a decent crust from the intense heat and seasoning.

I put it on a plate to rest while I deglazed the pan with some red wine.

The wine hissed against the heat, letting out a burst of tannic steam that caused my overly sensitive smoke detector to start blaring in alarm.

I left the steak for the moment and walked down to front foyer where the detector was affixed to the wall above a coat closet. I strained, reached up and pulled it from the wall to eliminate any further annoyances.

What I also knew was that both Giambone and McGeehan were vexed by the fact that I was asking questions.

That could be because they didn't want people probing their relationship too closely. Or it could be because they were powerful men who weren't used to having their actions questioned.

On the other hand, a pair of thugs that I believed was working for Giambone had landed me in the hospital for a few days. I couldn't prove a tie, but it did give my suppositions about their relationship a bit of credence.

Back in the kitchen, the red wine was bubbling happily as I scraped little bits of steak from the bottom of the pan.

I added a couple of tablespoons of butter and let that melt into the wine mixture while I rummaged some corn starch from a cup- board just below and to the right of the stove.

I added a bit of corn starch and whisked it until the sauce thickened.

When it looked to be getting too thick, I added a little more wine and the juices from the steak that had been resting on the counter.

So, I had the threads of connections between Giambone and McGeehan. I knew about the PAC and the non-profit in Bucks County.

What I still didn't know was why Peter Andre was dead. And I needed to know more if I was going to figure that part out.

As I mulled that over, I transferred the steak to a clean plate, added the fried potatoes and some microwaved green peas.

I spooned the finished wine sauce over the potatoes and the steak turned off the stereo and settled down in front of the TV to eat my dinner and watch a late-fall session of the Pennsylvania Senate on public-access cable.

As I chased the steak with sips of a decent, but cheap, bottle of red wine, the state Senate acted on bill that the clerk, a balding guy with glasses and Amish-looking beard, described in a bored monotone as "Senate Bill 452, legislation intended to encourage economic development in counties of the Second Class."

I had turned on the TV hoping to catch a glimpse of Lena, who'd been working late as the Legislature rushed to finish its work before the start of a two-week Thanksgiving Break.

It was paralyzingly boring. But even though I knew it was important stuff, I still fell asleep in my clothes heavy with red wine and a French bistro dish that an old girlfriend had taught me how to make.

When I woke the next morning, my head was fuzzy from the red wine, and the monotone-voiced Senate clerk was on a feedback loop inside my head.

I made a mental note to check out Senate Bill 452 when I got to the office.

CHAPTER 16

By my second cup of coffee the next morning, I was deep into the federal tax filings for the Greater Doylestown Development Corporation.

It was a cold and clear morning a few days before Thanksgiving, and the leaves were mostly off the trees now.

And the crisp cold of early fall was giving way to the damp, bone-clinging cold of early winter.

A half-finished cup of takeaway coffee sat on my desk next to a finished bag of Krispy Kreme donuts.

Only two. Don't worry. I'm watching myself.

I'd called Lena from the car, and she was still drowsy with sleep when she picked up.

"Did I wake you?" I asked as I made the left turn onto Market Street from Second during morning rush hour traffic. I maneuvered my trusty Saturn through the narrow lanes of traffic in front of the red brick-faced Whitaker Center, a local science museum and music hall that attracted B-level national touring acts. I'd seen Brian Wilson there a few years earlier.

"I don't know if you'd noticed," Lena returned. "But the Senate went kind of late last night."

"Believe it or not, I did," I said, as I tried, and failed, to balance the phone and my coffee, as well as steer, at the same time. I cursed as the steaming hot coffee splashed onto my leg.

"I stayed up late just to try to catch a glimpse of you," I said.

Lena laughed a charming, musical laugh, and said, "Why, Mr. Flynn, how very flattering. You decided to forgo sleep for little ole' me."

"Indeed, I did," I said. "You were to be the star that lit my night."

"Oh barf," she zinged back. "Nice try, though. I'll have to reward you tonight."

"Dinner?" I asked.

"Absolutely," she said. "Call me later?"

"You bet," I said. We said goodbye, I turned the music up.

It was already shaping up to be a good morning.

The federal 990 form for the Greater Doylestown Development Corporation still told me pretty much the same stuff it
had told me before. Namely, that it was still in Greater
Doylestown, and that Larry Keller, the district director for Sen.

J. Clarence McGeehan was still its executive director.

The tricky thing about nonprofits is that they aren't required to disclose their funding.

But they are required to disclose how they spend their
money. One of the beneficiaries, in this case, was a group
called Sunshine Properties LLC, based in Siesta Key, Fla.

There were about a dozen disbursements over the last year
or so.

All of them were in increments of $1,000 or $2,000. Not
enough to catch attention, but enough, if you added them up,
that they seriously started to matter.

A few clicks revealed that the Greater Doylestown Development Corp got a hefty chunk of change from the state
Department of Community Development, which was Pennsylvania's economic development agency.

It doled out grants, mostly politically motivated, to deserv-
ing groups.

For years, the rumor had been that state lawmakers used
the agency to reward their loyal supporters and block cap-
tains.

The grant from the state was a little bit more than
$500,000. About $50,000 of that was used to pay Larry Keller's salary as executive director. The rest of it went into
overhead and grant money for community groups in
Doylestown. One such worthy was a local softball league.

As I was glancing over the numbers, my head snapped
back. Keller was collecting a salary as executive director for

the community group, and, presumably, he was picking up a paycheck as McGeehan's district guy.

I picked up the phone and dialed our Capitol bureau.

Phil Lynette, the bureau chief, picked up on the second ring.

"Lynette," he grunted. In 10 years at the Banner, Lynette had picked up a reputation as a tireless digger who knew how to follow the money just about better than anyone else in the Capitol press corps.

It was his reporting that had led to revelations that legislative leaders had rewarded staffers who did political work with taxpayer-funded bonuses totaling around $5 million.

Those stories, in turn, had led to a statewide grand jury, and indictments for two, senior state House leaders. The cases were to go to trial the following year.

I was pretty sure that the paper now paid for someone to start Lynette's car and taste his food, but I could never prove it.

"Phil, it's Sean Flynn," I said. "You still got that printout of Senate staff salaries?"

"Yeah," he said. "Whaddya need?"

"Can you check the salary for a guy named Larry Keller? He's the district guy for Clarence McGeehan."

"Hang on," Lynette said, and I heard him grunt as he reached for something. Then I heard the flipping of pages.

"Keller ... Keller ... Keller ...," he muttered to himself. "Yep, here it is. He's making $85,000 this year."

I whistled.

"What's up? You got something?" Lynette asked.

"Phil, who's the best-paid state employee?" I asked him.

"That's easy," Lynette shot back. "It's the chief justice of the state Supreme Court. He makes just a shade under two-hundred grand."

"Who's the second-best paid?" I asked.

"The governor," Lynette said. "He makes about a buck-fifty a year."

I laughed.

"What?" Lynette demanded.

"Sonuvabitch," I said. "I do believe we just found the third-best-paid state employee.

"No, we haven't Flynn," Lynette said scornfully. "The guy only makes $85K. That's about as much as the governor's press secretary."

"Phil," I said slowly. "That's not his only salary." "Whaddya mean?"

I told him.

"Goddamn," he said.

"Uh-hunh," I said. "Philly, me lad. I do believe we have the beginnings of an actual scoop here. You want in?" "Are you kidding?" Lynette said.

"Good," I said. "Give me an hour to clear the desk on this car-crash story I've been working on. They only gave me 10 inches for it. Should be finished in no time flat."

"I'll be here," Lynette said.

Then I went off to find some editors so I could explain to them why I was working on a story I wasn't supposed to be working on anymore.

Vic Young wasn't really psyched.

On the other hand, he knew a good story when he saw it.

He went and told the higher-ups, who disappeared into a conference room for an hour while I put the finishing touches on the car-crash story.

They emerged with grim faces.

"Write it," Vic told me.

And we did.

CHAPTER 17

It was after 11 p.m. when I finally closed the top on my laptop, fastened the snaps on my leather satchel and eased myself into my coat.

The night desk guys were still at work and would be for at least two more hours until the paper's final deadline. In five short hours, the story I'd co-written with Phil Lynette would be landing on doorsteps across the Susquehanna Valley.

I'd briefly contemplated the possibility that the story might also land me a return visit from one of Rocco Giambone's goons. And I wasn't particularly in the mood for getting my ass kicked again, even if I did think that the scar above my right eyebrow did lend me a kind of rakish, Steve McQueen-like charm.

Apparently, Bernie O'Neill, the Banner's executive editor and a few of the day and night-side editors, including Vic Young and Eddie Drake, had been thinking along similar lines.

So maybe that's why I wasn't surprised to see a Harrisburg city police cruiser parked across the street from my house when I got home ten or so minutes later.

I'd called Lena earlier in the evening to cancel our dinner. She'd been remarkably understanding about the whole thing, considering it had been some time since we'd last seen each other. But we were working types and were used to having to put career in front of any number of other priorities.

Encouragingly, however, she had asked me to give her a call when I was getting ready to leave. She'd playfully mentioned something about a late dessert. I'd called her from the car on the way home, and she said she was on her way.

I pulled my car onto the narrow parking pad near my front door and locked the car behind me.

As I crossed the street, I could make out the profile of a young beat cop, Denny Truelock, in the low light of the street-lamp above the blue and yellow cruiser.

We didn't know each other well, but Denny had always been a decent sort when we'd had occasion to deal with each other.

He was, overall, refreshingly free of the cocky attitude that seems to infect young cops who deal with reporters.

Denny heard my footfalls as I crossed the street and looked up from the laptop that was casting a bluish glow on the front of his uniform shirt.

"Denny," I said, nodding to him as he stepped out of the car.

Denny Truelock was just a shade above six feet, and he wore his hair in a tight, quarter-inch crew cut that ended in a sharp line over his ears. His face was narrow and his alert eyes were spaced closely together.

He wasn't big, but he was lean.

And I was left with the distinct impression that he'd won more fights than he'd lost.

I knew he was from Carlisle, a town about 30 minutes south of Harrisburg down Interstate 81. He wasn't married. And at the age of twenty-six, that probably wasn't a bad thing, either.

"Mr. Flynn," he said, extending a hand as I drew close.

Denny was as tightly coiled as a spring. There was a palpable energy about him.

"How are you?"

"Not bad," I said. "You parked in front of the house because you like the river view and the quiet time it gives you to catch up on paperwork? If I'd known you were gonna be here, I would have put some coffee on."

Denny smiled, showing very white, very small teeth. He shook his head.

"Nice of you to offer, but I got a thermos and some sandwiches in the car," he said. "You probably know what I'm doing here."

I nodded, looking out across the river, which was flowing silently and eternally under the elaborate brickwork of the South Bridge, as it moved to complete a 444-mile-long journey that began at Otswego Lake near Cooperstown and ended in the Chesapeake Bay at Havre de Grace in Maryland.

"You're here for me," I said evenly. "I'm sure the good people of Harrisburg would love to know that their tax dollars are being used to keep an ink-stained wretch such as myself safe from the clutches of evil-doers. Who made the call?"

Denny Truelock spat onto the sidewalk.

"Your publisher called the chief. The chief called my shift commander. My shift commander called me. And here, as they say, I find myself."

"And how long is this supposed to continue?" I asked.

"Until quitting time for me," he said. "For you, I guess it continues until everyone's satisfied that you're not gonna wake up with a horse's head in bed with you."'

"Good to know," I said.

We both looked over our shoulders in the direction of gravel crunching on the sidewalk behind us. Lena materialized beside me and gave me a gentle kiss on the cheek.

"I don't see any dessert," I teased her, returning the kiss.

"It's inside," she said, jerking her head in the direction of my front door as Denny Truelock groaned.

"My bodyguard's here, Denny," I said. "I think I'll be perfectly safe now."

Denny nodded; his eyes filled with an easy mirth.

"G'night, Flynn," he said, then inclined his head in the direction of Lena, who was leading me by the hand across the street to my house. "Ma'am."

"Good night, officer," Lena said as we walked away.

"Hell of a job," Denny Truelock muttered to himself as he got back into his car. "Hell of a job."

CHAPTER 18

The next morning, Lena and I were sipping coffee at my kitchen counter as a cold and bright late-November sun streamed through the window above the sink.

She was still blinking the sleep from her eyes. And her lovely, strawberry blonde hair was piled haphazardly on top of her head.

She was wearing an old R.E.M. tour t-shirt that I'd picked up during the 1995 Monster tour.

When she leaned and turned against the counter to follow my progress with breakfast, the shirt stretched tight over her right side, accentuating the stunning curve of her hip.

To keep her lower half warm, she'd raided my closet for an old pair of sweatpants. They were a size or two, too big, and to keep them from slipping, she'd folded over the waist a couple of times, exposing her flat stomach, and the tiny jewel that nestled in her navel.

"If you keep doing that," I said, glancing up briefly from the quick fry-up of potatoes, eggs, and chorizo that I was preparing, "we may never get out of here."

Lena smiled broadly. It was a cute gesture that made her eyes crinkle charmingly and lit up her face. She did a little twirl and held her arms up like a game-show model.

"You like?" she asked.

I looked at her appreciatively and tried to concentrate on not burning breakfast.

"I don't think that R.E.M. shirt ever had it so good," I said, as I walked to the fridge and fished out a bag of shredded cheddar cheese to sprinkle over the contents of my cast-iron pan.

Lena left the counter that separated my kitchen from the living room and began browsing her way through a rack of compact discs that took up most of one wall.

"This is quite a collection," she said, her eyes traveling slowly over the line of jewel cases that stretched for about four feet between two sets of bookcases. She slowed as she browsed.

"Sean?" she asked.

"Yeah?" I called, removing the food from the heat as the cheese bubbled. I took two plates from a cabinet above my head and spooned the contents of the pan onto them.

"Are these CDs ... alphabetized?" Lena asked.

"Yep," I said, putting the two plates down on a small bistro table in my breakfast nook. I poured out two glasses of cranberry juice and splashed some coffee into two bone-china mugs that I'd bought at a restaurant supply house. I liked the hefty, diner-like feel of the cups and the black stripe that ran around the lip of each one.

"And they're sub-sorted by release date," I added.

Lena glanced at me sideways. "You're scaring me," she said. I shrugged.

"Sorry. A holdover from my college radio days, I guess. My sophomore year, I worked as program director. We had a huge library and it was the best way I could think of to organize stuff. Makes it that much easier to find."

Appropriate to the t-shirt, Lena pulled R.E.M.'s "Murmur" from the rack and inserted it into the CD-player that sat in a smoked glass cabinet beneath my television set.

A moment or two later, the opening strains of "Radio Free Europe," were blaring through my first floor.

Lena sat down at the table across from me and tucked her right leg under her left. She poked at her breakfast with a fork.

"And what do you call this?" she asked.

"The breakfast of champions," I said, chewing the corner off a piece of rye toast that I'd made to go with the fry-up. "It'll put a spring in your step and hair on your chest."

"Sean, there's enough cholesterol in here to drop a rhino," Lena whined.

I pointed my fork at her.

"Quiet. Eat. It's a cold day, and this'll keep you going until lunchtime."

Lena took a careful bite, chewed and then smiled contentedly as she finished.

"That's wonderful," she said. "It tastes so good that it can't possibly be good for me."

"It's not," I said. "But eat it anyway."

And we did, as we chatted away about our families, our plans for the holidays, and what we might do together later that week. There was no rush. The morning was about as perfect as it could get.

When we were almost finished, Lena extended one finely boned hand across the table and covered mine. It was tough work trying to eat and drink coffee with one hand, but hers felt so soft on top of mine that I couldn't bear to ruin the moment.

Later, while we were doing dishes, I asked her about the economic development legislation that I'd seen the Senate act on the night before.

"What can you tell me about Senate Bill 452?" I asked her.

Lena shrugged.

"No idea," she said. "They introduce something 1,500 bills during every two-year session. I'd have to look it up. Can I use your computer?"

"Sure," I said, pointing down the hall to the spare bedroom that I'd converted into a home office. "Please excuse the mess."

Lena disappeared down the hallway. As I finished the dishes, I could hear the tapping of computer keys.

"Sean," she called. "Come on down here."

I threw the towel on the counter, left the dishes in the plastic drying rack and walked to join her.

In the half-light of my office, Lena's face was illuminated by the glow of my laptop. She'd pulled up some kind of legislative Web site, and, and was staring intently at line after line of legalese.

"It's an economic development bill specifically for second-class counties," she said.

"I'd gathered that," I said as I hooked a chair to sit down beside her.

Our thighs were touching, and my breath came up a little short. We hadn't showered yet, and her hair had the fading smell of jasmine mixed with the warmth of sleep. "Won't those counties develop a complex if you call 'em second class?"

Lena grinned and elbowed me in the ribs.

"Cute. But the classification is based on population. Philly and Allegheny are considered first-class counties because of their size. A bunch of the suburban counties are Class Two. She toggled down.

"See, there's a list of them right here," she said.

I glanced down the list and almost jumped out of my seat when I saw the name of one of them.

"Lena," I asked. "How much money does this legislation appropriate?"

"I dunno. Usually, they just write enabling legislation, and then there's a separate bill that actually authorizes the specific amounts."

She tapped a few more keys, revealing a list of neat columns that had the name of the county on the left and the amounts in the right.

I glanced down the list, my eyes stopping in the same place as it had on the previous screen. I swallowed hard.

"What's the total appropriation for the bill?" I asked.

Lena scrolled up the screen to a summary paragraph that started the list of counties.

"Here it is," she said. "In total, it's one-point-five billion."

"Holy cats," I said. "That's a shed-load of cash."

"Yep," she said. "And the thing about these bills is that they're usually political payback for the folks back home. You know what they call it around the Capitol?"

"No, what's that?" I asked.

"'Mad Money'," Lena said, as she leaned back in my office chair and rested her head on my shoulder. She whispered sadly. "They treat it like it's their own."

One-point-five billion, I thought as we sat there in the early morning quiet. And now I knew where most of it was going.

CHAPTER 19

Larry Keller was a paunchy, red-faced guy with white hair whose prodigious chins spilled out over the top of a tartan plaid sport shirt.

His brown hair was parted just above his right ear and swooped dramatically over the top of his head and plastered into place.

We were sitting in his cramped cubicle on the first floor of Sen. J. Clarence McGeehan's district office in Doylestown.

The town's Main Street was lined with houses that looked like they'd been designed in consultation from the same folks who'd given us Cinderella's Castle.

That meant a profusion of pastel colors, carved curlicues on roof cornices, sprawling front porches, neatly trimmed trees and lawns so immaculately kept that they had hospital corners.

The little boutiques and restaurants that settled comfortably between those houses had also done everything they could to call attention to their saccharine sweetness – and their exclusiveness.

One bistro proudly advertised its three Michelin stars. A salon boasted of treatments that had recently been brought in from Europe. On the street, Volvos parked behind BMWs.

The town fathers, all too aware of their community's inherent adorableness, had done everything they could to make sure that it had calcified into law. The community was famed for having some of the most restrictive zoning rules in the country.

I was trying not to call attention to myself as I nosed my car into a spot in a public parking lot behind the distressed gingerbread building that housed McGeehan's district offices.

And if I was lucky, no one would notice that the Brooks Brothers shirt I was wearing had come from an outlet store.

But if I was out of place in tony Doylestown, then Larry Keller was like a Great Dane in a studio apartment.

The corners of his mouth were flecked with powdered sugar from the jelly donut he'd devoured while crossing the distance from the entrance to his cubicle to his desk.

The recently departed donut's lonely sibling sat on a bed of waxed paper beside a phone book on Keller's grease-stained desk blotter. It wasn't long for this world either.

"You're Flynn," he barked, jerking his head toward me and regarding me with piggish, brown eyes.

"Yep," I said, as I lowered myself into a chair across from Keller's desk. As I sat, something that felt like a spring jabbed itself into my butt. I made a mental note to get a tetanus shot when I got back to Harrisburg later that day.

Keller said nothing as I winced at the sharp pain of the spring.

He jammed half the second donut in his mouth and washed it down with a cream-slicked cup of take-out coffee.

"You wanna tell me why I should talk to you?" he demanded through a full mouth, as he sprayed crumbs and powdered sugar onto his shirtfront.

I took a notebook and pen from my pocket and flipped it open to a blank page.

"Because I'm such a charming devil?" I asked.

"Fuck you," Keller said. "You know how much shit I took when you wrote your little fucking story about me?"

I put up my hands in mock-surrender, but my eyes sent a different message entirely. I felt heat rise up my neck to my face and my heart beat a little faster. I swallowed back the anger and continued.

"I'm not sure how that's my fault," I said. "I'm not the one collecting two salaries. Nor do I have a job that seems to present an inherent conflict of interest."

Keller stared at me.

"You wanna tell me how it is you managed to swing two gigs that pay you almost as much as the governor?" I asked him.

Then he glared at me.

"Fuck you," he said again.

I shrugged.

"Okay, let me guess," I said. "You're a life-long political hack. Maybe you knew McGeehan when you were in high school? You two are about the same age, right?"

Again, Keller said nothing. But it looked like I was getting somewhere, so I kept at it.

"I bet you worked your way up from ward-heeler to precinct-captain. You probably found that you liked the work. It wasn't that hard. And McGeehan's probably the sort who rewards loyalty, right?

Across the desk from me, Keller leaned back in his seat and crossed his hands across his chest. His eyes had narrowed, and he was regarding me with an indifference that was rapidly crossing over to hostility.

"After a couple of years, you were probably running his reelects, and then, after a while, McGeehan gave you this place to run. The pension's ironclad. The benefits are free. And after 25 years, you get to retire, right? This is probably the best job you've ever had. Hell, it's probably the only job you've ever had."

Across the desk from me, Keller's breath was coming in short bursts. His face had gone from red to purplish as I wrapped up my tale and his tiny eyes were stabbing daggers into my chest.

"Any of that sound right?" I asked.

"Fuck you," he said, hoarsely. "Get out of my office."

He stood up in his chair. He was maybe five-foot-nine in heels, and he was old and out-of-shape, but you could tell he was used to people listening to him when he talked. But it probably wasn't him that people feared. It was his boss.

It was an old story. Keller was just another one of those who'd confused his proximity to power with actual power. He only had as much clout as his boss was willing to give him.

But even if I knew all of that was true, I wasn't exactly in the mood to go twelve rounds with a guy cruising towards seventy and his second heart attack.

He was standing chest-to-chest with me now. I had him by maybe three inches and ten pounds. If he tried something, he wasn't going to come out at the right end of it.

"I said, 'Get the fuck out of my office,'" Keller repeated.

I backed away, tucked my notebook into my back pocket and slipped the pen into the bomber jacket I was wearing.

"I didn't come here looking for a fight, Larry," I said. "I came here looking for information."

"Well, you goddamned well found a fight," Keller shot back. "Now, screw."

Unable to think of anything else to do, I screwed, leaving Keller standing in the entrance to his cubicle as sweat dribbled down his face and a secretary stared after me in amazement.

"Have a good day," I told her.

CHAPTER 20

While not a complete success, my little jaunt to the Philadelphia suburbs hadn't been an abject failure either.

For one thing, I'd managed to annoy a lifelong political hack, so that wasn't exactly a day wasted. For another, I was also finding that the more I tugged on the loose ends in Sen. J. Clarence McGeehan's life, the more he, or someone who worked with him, tried to pull the ends tighter.

That was some consolation, I thought, as I pulled off Route 611 in Montgomery County near the now-closed Willow Grove Naval Air Station, past a row of chain restaurants and cookie-cutter bargain hotels, and onto the westbound lane of the Pennsylvania Turnpike.

It was a cold day, getting colder, and the sky was clouding with what could have been the season's first snow. I'd always been an autumn guy. I liked the sense that things were changing, the crisp snap to the air when you breathed it in.

But that autumn only lasted until, maybe, the end of October, before the clinging damp of November overtook it with a vengeance that settled into your bones and sent you scurrying for the protection of a roaring fire and cups of mulled cider.

I had an Elvis Costello compilation playing through the Bluetooth. And I sang along loudly as Declan and the boys ripped into "Radio, Radio."

I listened as Bruce Thomas and Pete Thomas beat out the rhythm on bass and drums, respectively, and then marveled at the keyboard prowess of Steve Nieve, who wrung a wall of whining noise out of his Vox organ like his life depended on it.

It was around the Valley Forge exit, near where the highway split onto Route 202 and the King of Prussia Mall when I finally noticed the black Cadillac Escalade that took up most of my rearview mirror.

Either the driver was a nervous Nellie – he accelerated when I accelerated and slowed down when I slowed down – or I was the victim of one of the worst tail jobs in history.

With Elvis soulfully crooning away on "Every Day I Write the Book," I decided to test my theory.

Every couple hundred yards, I'd switch from the right lane into the left lane. And sure enough, my erstwhile traveling companion would execute a similar lane switch.

This clumsy game of cat-and-mouse continued along the 45-minute length of the Turnpike through Montgomery and Chester counties. The Elvis Costello compilation gave way to the Dream Syndicate's "The Days of Wine and Roses," a dark and brooding record that reflected not only the weather but also my souring mood.

As we rushed along, my eyes alighted on a road sign warning of a rest area just two miles ahead.

I made the snap decision to pull in, guessing, correctly, I hoped, that whoever was driving the Escalade wouldn't be stupid enough to pull anything in a crowded public place.

When we reached the rest area, I nosed my car into a parking place near the front of the low, brick-faced building that housed a couple of fast-food joints and a Starbucks stand.

A short distance beyond the building, a Sunoco gas station sold gas for twenty-five cents-a-gallon more than you'd pay at a station off the Turnpike.

I'd never understood how the mark-up worked.

Assuming I lived long enough, I made a note to ask our transportation reporter about it the next time I saw him.

Of course, it might be hard to form a question with my jaw wired shut, but hope sprang eternal.

The Escalade pulled into a spot two car lengths behind mine, next to a crowded Dodge minivan filled with screaming kids and young parents who wore that universal, put-upon look that all parents seemed to wear. It wasn't a look of surrender exactly. It was more like one of resignation.

The father was wearing a Penn State warm-up jacket that was maybe a size too small for him. His belly strained against the insulated nylon fabric as he struggled to latch one of his brood into her car seat.

The toddler cried as she grabbed for a toy that lay just ou of reach.

And I heard her father gently tell her he'd give it to her once she was settled into her seat.

The mother, meanwhile, expertly lashed their second child, also a girl, into her car seat.

She was probably somewhere around thirty, with long, black hair that she'd tied back into a ponytail away from a pale, white face.

Her eyes were blue, and there were hints of freckles around the bridge of her nose.

Her jersey fit her snuggly. And though her husband seemed like he had given up the fight against advancing years and a slowing metabolism, she clearly had not.

I was walking toward the doors of the rest stop when I saw two men climb out of the Escalade in a way that suggested that they weren't trying to call attention to themselves.

I recognized them immediately as the twin thugs who'd worked me over when Lena and I had been walking along the river a few weeks earlier.

It was light out this time, and I had enough time and distance to memorize their features.

If I was still able to talk when this encounter ended, I figured it'd be nice if I could offer a description to the cops.

The thug twins followed me into the rest stop and pretended to browse at a magazine rack while I got into line at Starbucks.

Ahead of me, an older woman, mystified by the array of choices presented to her, took a good ten minutes to decide between a large mocha and a small vanilla cappuccino.

Ultimately, she went with a small, regular coffee, with room for cream, and the world continued to spin on its axis.

Around her, the caffeine junkies muttered darkly and swore strange oaths.

When I got to the front of the line, the elaborately tattooed young woman behind the counter wore a look of fear. Would I put her through the same hell? I did not, and briskly ordered my grande coffee.

Did they have the Sumatra? They did?

Excellent. And yes, room for cream, please.

The barista sighed with relief.

I paid her and went to a side counter where I added some cream and two sugars to the steaming, take-away cup.

I was about to splash in a bit of grated nutmeg when I felt a pair of heavy hands on my shoulders. I didn't have to turn around. I knew who it was.

Thug One, looking exactly as I remembered him from our encounter on the river, whispered hoarsely in my ear.

"Don't even fucking think about trying to call for help or make a break for it, reporter-boy. Pull any shit, and we'll kill you right here."

"I wouldn't even dream of it," I said. "Besides, I've been kind of missing you guys. Life's been a little empty without you around."

I turned around slowly, one hand on the uncovered cup of Starbuck's coffee.

The thug twins were standing, maybe, three of four inches away from me. The first one, I judged him to be the older of the two, had a placid expression and a scar above his right eye.

His hair was combed back from his forehead and there was a few days' worth of stubble on his chin.

The second was just as tubby as I remembered him. And he once again wore some kind loose-fitting warm-up jacket that only served to call attention to the fact that he was fat and getting fatter.

Even still, he had a look that suggested he had once been strong, and I was under no illusions about their capacity for cruelty.

"Here's how it's gonna work," Thug Two said as pleasantly as if we were discussing traffic conditions or the best place to score a hot dog. "You're gonna' walk with us into the bathroom, and when we get there you are gonna' get a severe talking-to."

Thug One chimed in, "Try anything stupid. Try to run. And we'll hunt you down, and we'll kill you. It's that simple."

I swallowed – hard – as I looked at the two of them

"Why should I believe that you're just not going to kill me in the bathroom?" I asked.

"You can't," the second thug said. "But we've already told you what will definitely happen to you if you try to make a break for it."

I nodded, considering my choices.

"Is there a third choice?" I asked.

The two leg-breakers looked at each other and grinned.

"He's pretty funny, isn't he, Phil?" the second thug asked his partner.

"He thinks he's funny," Phil said coldly. "But he won't be laughing for long."

While the two thugs were talking, I noticed a Pennsylvania State Police trooper walk through the rest-area's double-doors, pass under the skylight at the center of the room, and get in line at a burger stand.

I had maybe one shot at this. The choice was run and die. Or go into the bathroom and maybe get drowned in a toilet.

And there was no way I was gonna explain that one to H.L. Mencken when I met him on the other side. There was no way I was gonna spend eternity in Reporter's Heaven as Drowned-in-the-Toilet-Guy.

The two thugs stopped their laughing and stared at me. Thug One, Phil, jerked his head in the direction of the men's room.

"Let's go," he said. I shook my head. "Unh-uh," I said.

One of Phil's meaty hands landed on my shoulder and he jerked me forward.

"I said, 'Let's go,'" he repeated.

As he did that, I hit him full in the face with the open cup of coffee. Phil screamed as the scalding hot liquid covered his head and ran down into his eyes.

The second thug whirled on me.

"You are so gonna regret that, you little motherfucker," he growled.

Ducking low, I kicked him, as hard as I could in the groin.

I heard the air whoosh out of him as I connected. He doubled over in pain.

"Should have worn a cup," I said, as he clutched himself, and Phil writhed in agony on the floor.

Around me, people were screaming, and, as if in slow motion, I saw teenaged clerks crouch in terror behind their fast-food counters.

At the burger stand, the trooper sprang into action in one fluid move.

I felt my legs go out from under me as he tackled me, and my face connected with the cold of the tiled floor. My arms were jerked behind me, and I heard the click of his handcuffs.

The trooper was barking something into the radio hand-piece clipped to the shoulder of his uniform blouse. And before I knew it, two other troopers burst through the double- doors, leveling their sidearms at the fallen thugs.

"Don't move," said the trooper who'd tackled me. "Don't even breathe."

I didn't.

I was under arrest.

But at least I was alive.

CHAPTER 21

Four hours later, I was sitting in a conference room of a Pennsylvania State Police substation in Chester County. It was the nearest station to the rest stop. And they'd taken me there after my face-off with the Thug Twins.

The trooper who'd cuffed me, the nametag on his uniform blouse read "Bettini," thrust me into the back of his cruiser. Thugs One and Two were taken away in handcuffs by the two troopers that Bettini had radioed for back-up.

Bettini had thick, curly hair and a five o'clock shadow. He was about my height and probably a few years older than me. There was a platinum wedding band on his left hand and the polished black of his boots matched the butt of the gun that sat on his left hip.

My little stunt at the rest stop had worked. Sure, it had gotten me arrested, but it had worked. Phil, Thug 1, had first degree burns on his face, and his buddy probably wouldn't be dating for a while.

On the other hand, as bad as things were for them, they could have come out far worse for me.

The rest stop had emptied out quickly while the state cops interviewed witnesses – including the Starbucks barista who had sold me my life-saving cup of joe.

"You all right back there?" Bettini asked over his shoulder when he pulled the cruiser into traffic.

"As well as can be expected, I guess," I told him.

He grunted and nodded and then we drove in silence with only the pop and crackle of the police radio to keep us company.

At the station, I was booked, photographed and fingerprinted.

To my eternal relief, my insurance and registration were up-to-date, and I didn't have any outstanding warrants. On the other hand, the state cops did take some glee from the mountain of unpaid parking tickets I owed to the city of Harrisburg.

"You'll really need to pay those," Bettini said, as he led me, with my hands cuffed behind my back, down the hall to a conference room.

I passed the two thugs in the hallway. Phil had bandages on his face, and he glared at me through angry eyes.

His partner scowled and looked away.

Bettini led me through two or three turns, deep into the bowels of the station, past secretaries sitting at their desks and past an assembly room where troopers gathered at the beginning of their shifts.

Taking an electronic card key from his pocket, Bettini opened a heavy, wooden door marked "Conference Room A," and led me inside.

At the end of the conference table nearest to the door, a plainclothes investigator who introduced himself later as "LaCaprucia" looked up as Bettini led me to the other end of the table and dropped me, just gently enough, into a chair.

"Are you enjoying that?" I asked him, as my butt collided with the cold metal of a folding chair.

"Enjoying what?" he asked, the corners of his mouth turned up with mirth.

"Playing the hard-case cop," I returned.

"Just trying to give you the authentic law-enforcement experience," Bettini said. "I know how much you reporters love those tiny details for your stories."

LaCaprucia barked.

"Enough," he said. "Let's get this started."

I glanced across the table at him.

"Speak," he said.

I did.

LaCaprucia listened in silence to everything I told him as he took notes with a No. 2 pencil on a yellow legal pad in a spidery hand.

I judged LaCaprucia to be about fifty. He had a narrow, dark Italian face with dark circles under his eyes. His mustache, thick, and flecked with gray, was neatly trimmed.

His tie was loose, and a gray flannel suit jacket hung over the back of his chair. I didn't look, but I knew his trousers matched.

The walls of the conference room were painted a sickly public-school green. Affixed to the walls were faded law enforcement posters, yellowed with age, exhorting kids not to do drugs and encouraging citizens to give to the Police Athletic League.

At the far end of the room, behind LaCaprucia, was the standard one-way glass.

Bettini, the trooper, stood behind LaCaprucia at the door, his arms folded over his chest. His eyes betrayed no expression.

"Harrisburg cops speak well of you," LaCaprucia said.

"I like to think it's my winning personality," I said.

He laughed mirthlessly.

"Now tell me what happened again," he said. "This is a hell of a thing you got yourself into."

And I did, once more spooling out all the details from Peter Andre's death the previous summer to what I'd uncovered about the Pennsylvania Better Government Association and the Greater Doylestown Development Corporation.

I also told LaCaprucia about my earlier encounters with the two goons and how their first visit had landed me in the hospital.

LaCaprucia kept taking notes, and, when I paused, he nodded at me to continue.

An hour later, we were done, and around us, sat the wreckage of empty cups of coffee and bags of snacks that LaCaprucia had asked one of his staff to bring into the conference room.

"You understand, of course, that we're going to have to charge you with disturbing the peace and assault?" he said, tucking the pencil into his suit coat pocket as he picked up his legal pad as he got up to leave.

"I do," I said.

LaCaprucia reached into the inner pocket of his suit coat and dropped a business card on the table.

"You remember anything else, or learn something new, call this number," he said.

He turned to the trooper.

"Andy," he said. "Take the cuffs off. Clark Kent here is free to go."

Bettini crossed behind his boss and walked to my end of the table. I heard the click of the handcuffs and felt the needles and pins in my wrists where the cuffs had bit into them, "Thank you," I told Bettini, as I rubbed my wrists to encourage circulation again.

LaCaprucia looked at me.

"You're onto something here," he said. "You do your part and we'll do ours."

I nodded and nearly asked a question.

Sensing what I wanted to ask, LaCaprucia provided an answer.

"The two goons who grabbed you had warrants in Monroe and Montgomery counties. They'll be guests of the legal system for a while, so you won't have to worry about them."

"Good to know," I told him. "As much as I enjoyed the attention, I was getting a little tired of all these people trying to kick my ass."

LaCaprucia nodded and looked me up and down once more.

"Remember to show up for your court date," he said.

I nodded.

As he opened the door, LaCaprucia gave me a last look.

"And Flynn?" he asked. "Yeah?"

"This may be difficult for you --- but try not to get yourself killed."

Then he was gone, and Bettini, the trooper, and I were alone in the room. He smiled widely.

"What?" I asked him.

"You keep this up, you may want to learn how to fight," he said. "I'd be embarrassed if I got my ass kicked so many times."

He did have a point.

CHAPTER 22

And so, a few days later, I was standing in the gymnasium at the Masonic Temple up on Third Street. Marty Herman, clad in running shoes, sweatpants and gray Harrisburg Police Department t-shirt, stood across from me.

It was three weeks before Christmas.

Outside, the season's first snow covered the ground. The walls of the temple, ancient and dark wood, were hung with plastic garlands and imitation pine wreaths. Somewhere, a radio played old Christmas carols.

Dean Martin's version of "Let It Snow," echoed through the building.

I looked around the room at the ancient Shriners who worked as volunteers. The building was a grand art deco space designed by a noted Harrisburg architect named Charles Howard Lloyd.

It had taken two years to build. Construction started in 1928.

And by 1930, the Shriners had a place to call their own in a part of the city that had once been considered exclusive.

Behind a counter on the far wall, three aged Shriners worked the snack bar, serving up coffee and bad jokes to all comers.

I glanced at them.

"You suppose they got here on those little motorcycles?" I asked him.

Marty Herman ignored me. But his eyes danced merrily, and his face creased into a grin.

"So, let me get this straight," he said. "You want me to teach you how to box."

"Yep," I said, as we walked into the locker room and began to change.

"You. Want. Me. To. Teach. You. How. To Box," he said again, slowly this time, drawing out each word into a sentence.

I nodded.

"Let's just say that my latest experience with the criminal underworld convinced me that it was a good idea," I said as I inspected my physique and compared it to Marty's.

He was a full head taller than me, and I don't think there was an ounce of spare fat anywhere on him. There was a tattoo on his left shoulder, some kind of Chinese character, and a scar on his right.

Over drinks one night, he'd told me how he'd got it. His skin stretched tight over his biceps. The cloth of his sweatpants strained against his thighs.

I was definitely lacking.

My gut spilled over the edge of my sweatpants, and spindly arms hung at my sides.

Sure, I kept in decent shape by running. But all that would get me was a significant head start before the bad guys finally caught me and kicked my ass again.

"It's gonna be hard work," Marty said as he led me into the main gym.

"I know," I said, as I looked around. Free weight machines were arranged in a hollow square around mirrored walls. In the middle of the square, two heavy bags were suspended from a low beam that ran the length of the room.

At the far end of the wall was a pair of speed bags.

A young Hispanic kid, probably no more than seventeen or eighteen was working one of the speed bags when we came in.

He beat a solid rhythm on the bag, making it sing with a blinding array of punches. I could have sworn he was whistling.

If he knew we were there, he ignored us.

"So how did your bosses take your adventures in law enforcement?" Marty asked me as he leaned against the ropes, stretching.

I laced my shoes for what seemed like the forty-second time. I hadn't been in a fight since grade school. And I was nervous about throwing punches.

"They used words like 'suspension,' 'probation,' and 'termination,'" I told him. "In the end, they settled for probation. I'm not supposed to get into trouble anymore. Something about how their insurance premiums are going through the roof because of me."

Marty grinned.

"And what about your court case?" he asked.

I shrugged.

"I must have gotten the most lenient magisterial district justice in Chester County. He decided I had sufficient reason to fear my life was in danger and was justified in my assault by Sumatra roast. He sentenced me to community service."

"What do you have to do?" Marty asked me.

"I have to go back and clean that rest stop in Chester County next weekend," I told him.

We laughed.

"All right, then. What's first?" I asked Marty as I picked up a pair of gloves that sat on a bench in front of us. The air stank of sweat and another radio was tuned to an album rock station.

Marty took the gloves out of my hand. "First," he said. "You put those down." He thrust a jump rope into my hands. "Ten minutes," he said.

I stared at him.

"You want me to jump rope?"

Marty glared at me.

"I jump rope," he said. "It's the best cardio training there is."

He picked up his own rope, and within seconds, it was whirring around his head. I could detect no change in his breathing.

I shrugged and tried to follow Marty Herman's lead. About all I succeeded in doing was wrapping the jump rope around my head. Marty Herman collapsed into paroxysms of laughter.

And at the far end of the room, the young Hispanic boy broke away from his speed bag. A wide smile crossed his face.

"Am I this afternoon's entertainment?" I asked Marty, who was trying to catch his breath.

He nodded.

"You are indeed," he said. Try again."

I did. And to my surprise, I managed to catch a rhythm. Within 10 or 15 minutes, I had a pretty good pace going and the front of my t-shirt was soaked through with sweat.

"That's enough," said Marty, who was sitting on a bench in front of me and watching my every move.

I stopped. My chest was heaving, and my eyes burned from the sweat that had poured down into them from my forehead. Marty handed me a water bottle. I took a long, greedy drink and settled onto the bench across from him.

He stared at me.

"What?" I asked him.

"You're serious about staying with this?" he asked. I nodded.

"Why?"

"How long we known each other?" I asked him.

"I dunno. Eight, maybe 10 years," he said. He wiped his neck and face with a towel that was slung over his shoulder.

"And, in all that time, have you ever known me to let go of a story once I have it?" I asked back, catching the towel as he threw it to me. I mopped my face and hair.

He shook his head.

"You are a stubborn sunovabitch," he said. "But I've never known you to stay on a story even if it meant getting landed in the hospital."

"That's the point," I said. "Now it's personal. If I let go now, they win. They've come at me three times, Marty."

"I know," he said.

"And once, they came at me when Lena was with me," I continued.

Marty gazed at me with appreciation.

"This is about Lena," he said. "Who knew you were such a romantic bastard?"

"It's about doing what's right," I told him. "It was your wife and kid, you'd do the same."

He nodded wordlessly and threw a pair of gloves at me.

They hit my stomach with a solid "thwump." "Put those on," Marty said.

CHAPTER 23

Two hours later, showered, shaved, and glowing with good health, Marty Herman and I slid into a booth at the Twin Fountains Diner on Second Street.

The kitschy music was blaring, as it always was, but at least this time, someone had had the foresight to make sure? and The Mysterians' "96 Tears" had made the rotation.

A waitress ambled over to take our order.

"What'll it be, boys?" she asked, hitting her mark perfectly.

Marty put down the menu without looking at it.

"Turkey sandwich," he said. "On rye. No mayo. Hold the tomato. And an iced tea, please."

The waitress looked at me. I thumbed the pages quickly.

"French Dip," I told her. "Diet Pepsi, please."

"Great choices, fellas," the waitress said, smiling widely at us. "I'll be back in a jiffy."

Marty stared after her.

"I do believe they call that method-acting," I told him.

"I don't care what they call it," he said. "She can do it whenever she wants."

"You're married, Marty," I reminded him.

"Doesn't mean I can't look, pal," he shot back.

I winced in pain as I tried shrugging out of my leather jacket. Marty heard me grunt and grinned.

"Yeah," he said. "It'll feel that way for a while." "My arms feel like lead," I told him.

The waitress reappeared with our drinks. She put the iced tea in front of me and the Diet Pepsi in front of Marty.

"Here you go, boys," she said, snapping her bubble gum as she walked away.

When she was out of sight, I switched our glasses.

"No one's perfect," Marty said.

"Indeed," I told him. "You're telling me that, eventually, I'll be able to use my arms again?"

He nodded as he squeezed a lemon into his tea and chased it with two packs of artificial sweetener from a caddy at the far end of the table.

"It's like everything else," he said. "It gets easier with practice."

I took a sip from my soda.

"All right," I told him, remembering the two hours of punch combinations on the heavy bag that Marty had shown me and my humiliation at the speed bag.

"I hope you're right," I said. "It does. Trust me."

"Humph," I snorted and turned my attention to my drink.

We sat in silence for a few minutes, each watching the pedestrian traffic on Second Street.

The waitress appeared with our food. She put Marty's lunch in front of me and mine in front of him.

"Ta-Da!" she announced with great flourish and a toothy smile. "Enjoy your lunch, boys."

Marty shook his head as she walked away.

"She's trying," I told him as we switched plates.

"Says you," he said, as he shook salt over his French fries. He picked one up, took a bite, and put it down. A look of revulsion crossed his face.

"Is it too late to tell you that they season the fries in the kitchen?" I asked him.

"You might have warned me," he said.

I shrugged, dunked my French Dip into a soup cup filled with *au jus* sauce and took a big bite. I chewed and swallowed.

"You didn't give me any time," I told him.

Marty looked sadly at his plate of fries.

"Now what am I gonna do?" he asked helplessly.

"You could always ask for another order," I offered.

"I do that, she might come back with deep-fried pickles," he said.

"You've got a point," I said and took another bite of sandwich.

Marty tucked into his turkey sandwich.

"What are you gonna do," he asked me, mid-mouthful as toast crumbs sprayed out of his open maw.

"About the story? Or about getting you some remedial table manner lessons?" I asked, wiping the front of my shirt where Marty's projectile crumbs had landed.

"What?" he asked through another mouthful.

I crinkled my nose in disgust.

"Some days, I wonder why Jeannie married you," I said.

"Me too," he retorted. "You gonna answer the question or what?"

I took another bite of my sandwich, chased it with the last of my Diet Pepsi, and signaled our waitress for a refill.

"Hell if I know," I told him. "The more I chase this thing, the less sense it makes to me.

"Lay it out for me again," Marty said.

"All right," I said. "Here's what I know. I know that Peter Andre is still dead – which is helpful because it remains constant. I know that the oh-so-cuddly Rocco Giambone gives heavily to the honorable Senator J. Clarence McGeehan's campaign, and that McGeehan's local chief-of-staff is the executive director of a non-profit run by Giambone."

Marty sat perfectly still as I spoke. He had a deadly serious look in his eye, and I knew that he was listening to each piece of information and turning it over in his mind.

It's what made him such a good cop. Underneath his tough-guy exterior lurked a very bright guy. Why he hadn't risen to detective by now always eluded me.

Marty motioned for me to continue. His sandwich sat, untouched, on his plate.

"And I know that the non-profit, an outfit called the Greater Doylestown Development Corporation, which gives to Giambone's PAC, is partially underwritten by state grant money and an outfit called Sunshine Properties LLC in Florida.

"Finally, I know that McGeehan is shepherding through a bill that would create a tax-break for second-class sized counties. And guess which one that is?"

"Bucks County," Marty said.

"And what's in Bucks County?" I asked.

"Doylestown," he said.

"Uh-hunh," I told him.

Marty picked up his sandwich, took a bite and chewed thoughtfully.

"So, where's that leave us?" I asked him.

He swallowed and took a sip of his iced tea.

"Two places,' he said, as he wiped his mouth from the napkin he'd placed in his lap at the beginning of our meal.

"First, we need to find out what McGeehan and Giambone have to gain from getting that bill through the Legislature," he said.

"And second?" I asked him.

"We need to find out what Sunshine Properties LLC is, and why it's donating so much money to a Pennsylvania nonprofit," he concluded.

"Are you suggesting we divide the labor?" I asked him. "Exactly that," Marty said.

"So how do we decide?" I asked him, finishing off my sandwich and rinsing it down with a final sip of Diet Pepsi. "Which of us has more vacation time?" Marty asked. I looked away.

"How much unused time, Sean?" he asked me. "Twenty-five days," I told him.

"Twenty-five days?" he repeated.

I shrugged, embarrassed.

"I don't get out much," I told him.

Marty signaled for the waitress.

"Don't forget to write," he told me.

CHAPTER 24

Three days later, Lena and I were driving south on Interstate 75 in a rented Volkswagen Passat toward Sarasota.

The car's air conditioner blasted us with cold air. We'd exited our flight from wintry Harrisburg to find Tampa unforgivingly humid -- even in mid-December. The temperature was in the low eighties. And within moments of getting off our too-crowded flight, we'd ditched our jackets and stuffed them in our carry-on luggage.

A packed monorail filled with weary tourists ferried us from our gate to the airport terminal.

We picked up our rental car in the bowels of the airport, suffering only a minimum of hassle from the harried twenty-something who chewed his lower lip in consternation as he clicked through menu after menu on an amber-screened computer monitor.

I'd cashed in the vacation time I had left for the year. And, to be honest, I think the paper was only too glad to be rid of me for a while.

Of course, I didn't tell them the real reason I was going to Florida. That would have only worried them further. And they might have tried to stop me.

Brent Vernet and I shook hands over our partition the day before I left.

"Have a good trip," he said. "And Merry Christmas."

"You, too," I told Vernet.

On the other side of the partition, Melanie Goslin smiled gently at me.

"Have a good trip, Sean," she said, as she tried to hand a small package, wrapped in holiday paper, over the partition to me.

I came around the other side to get it from her.

"What's this?" I asked.

"Just a little something to read on your flight," she said,

smiling.

I leaned in as she half embraced me.

"Thanks, Mel," I told her.

"You're welcome, Sean," she said. "Merry Christmas."

"Merry Christmas, Mel," I said. "I'll see you soon."

The book, a copy of Fitzgerald's 'Tender is the Night,' was in my carry-on, which sat on the backseat behind Lena on the passenger's side.

Lena's window was open, and the wind whipped her hair around her head.

She fiddled with the control of the radio and turned up the volume. I'd plugged my iPhone right after I turned on the ignition.

"What is this?" she asked, her brow creasing behind an enormous pair of sunglasses.

"It's a recording of John Peel's 'Festive 50' countdown from 1986," I said.

Blank stare.

"Very famous BBC dee-jay," I explained. "He's credited with helping to break a lot of the post-punk and indie artists of the late 1970s and early 1980s."

"Uh-hunh," Lena said. "And who are we listening to now?"

I cocked my head and listened.

"The Smiths," I told her. "The tune's called 'There is a Light That Never Goes Out.'"

"I like it," she said and turned to look out the window as Tampa Bay unfolded on both sides of us as we crossed the towering span of the Sunshine Skyway Bridge.

At its center point, the bridge looked like an enormous sail. The view of crystal-clear azure water was breathtaking.

The Smiths gave way to the "Age of Consent" by New Order, which soon gave way to Primal Scream and their indelible tune "Velocity Girl," a refreshing burst of jangle-pop that lasted all one minute and thirty seconds.

Lena shook her head in amusement.

"What?" I asked.

"Do you listen to anything recorded after 1992?" she demanded.

"Sure," I said. "Go ahead and scroll through. There's some Oasis in there. Some Snow Patrol. There might even be ... *gasp* ... some Coldplay."

Lena laughed a beautiful, lilting laugh.

"OK, allow me to rephrase," she said. "Do you listen to music not recorded by skinny white guys from England?"

"Not hardly," I said.

"Mmmm," she said. "And why not?"

"It's just the music I got into when I was younger," I told her. "Remember, I did some college dee-jaying just like you did. Except, when I did it, these were the records that were out. They just stuck with me."

"You're not going to tell that 'They don't make 'em like they used to,' are you?" she asked.

"Not hardly," I said.

She nodded in satisfaction.

"Good," she said.

A little more than an hour later, I pulled the rental car into the circular driveway of a little boutique hotel off the Avenue of the Arts in downtown Sarasota.

A valet in a red shirt and cap trotted over and efficiently opened my door. He was halfway around the car to help Lena before my feet hit the pavement.

The air was oppressively hu- mid, and a weak breeze blew in off the Gulf through a stand of palm trees that were the focal point of an immaculately landscaped island in the middle of the driveway.

We walked under a tan porte-cochere and into the hotel lobby.

The interior of the hotel was done up to look like someone's idea of tropical chic.

Gentle pastels abounded and the lobby walls were lined by Adirondack chairs painted a glistening white. The walls, above equally immaculately white wainscoting, were a pale blue.

We were greeted by a clerk with an Eastern European accent who efficiently processed our reservation and got us to our room.

I tipped the bellboy – his name was Adam -- after he deposited us and our bags in our room.

"Anything you need, Mr. Flynn," he said, as he backed out of the room. "You just let me know. I work until five most days, but I'm here all night tonight."

"I will," I said. "Thanks for your help."

"You're welcome sir," Adam said, pocketing the twenty I'd folded into his palm as we shook hands. "Any time at all."

Our room was on the tenth floor. And we were up high enough to see a marina from our window. Lena threw open the curtains and slid open the windows.

The room soon filled with the smell of the salt-scented air.

Lena turned and looked at me. Her green eyes seemed bottomless and her hair fell in gentle waves over her shoulders.

She smiled softly at me.

"Thanks for inviting me, Sean," she said. "I'm really happy to be here."

My breath caught in my throat as I stared at her. There had been plenty of women over the years. And, hell, I'd maybe even loved some of them.

And that included the marriage that came too young and washed up on the rocks just like the waves breaking on the jetty outside our hotel window.

But here, in this room, with this woman, the rest of the world melted away until all I could hear was her voice, and all I could see was her face coalescing, tranquil and beautiful, around her smile.

"You're welcome,' I stammered as she moved slowly across the room to me.

In a single movement, Lena pulled her t-shirt over her head and her bra, pale pink, fell to the floor. Her jeans followed.

"What are you waiting for?" she asked mischievously, as she smiled the same smile that the serpent probably used on Adam and Eve in the Garden.

I had no reasonable answer, so I followed suit.

Later, when we were done, the sheets were a tangle around us, and Lena and I lay, naked, over them. A ceiling fan whirred overhead.

Lena's head rested on my shoulder and rose and fell with my breathing.

We were silent for a few minutes. She broke it first.

"You're not going to spend the whole time we're here working, are you?" she asked. "I had to use my last vacation time to come here."

"No," I said. "I'm not. But I am going to spend tomorrow out on Siesta Key trying to figure out what Sunshine Properties is and what it does."

"What am I going to do?" she asked.

"I am going to leave you in a shopping district called St. Armand's Circle. Where I am sure, you will do what comes naturally. Then I'll join you for a late lunch, where I'll expose you to the genius that is the Cuban sandwich. Tomorrow night, we'll take in a show at the Van Wezel auditorium – that's an arts center near here – and we'll have a late supper in the hotel. And ..."

"And ... there's more?" Lena asked as she propped her chin on one hand and stared at me.

"And ..." I said. "If you are very lucky, I shall allow you to violate me again."

"Sounds wondrous," Lena said drily, as she kissed me quickly on the lips.

She hopped out of bed and headed toward the shower.

"But first, I require dinner."

"That can be arranged," I said, gazing appreciatively after her.

Lena gave her hips some extra swing when she reached the bathroom door.

"You going to join me?" she asked, her bangs falling, peek-aboo style, over her eyes like Veronica Lake in "The Blue Dahlia."

"Absolutely," I said.

Dinner was later than we thought.

CHAPTER 25

At ten the next morning, Lena and I were back in the rental car, crossing a causeway into St. Armand's Circle on a street called John Ringling Boulevard.

Midway across, we paused at a drawbridge, and watched, in wonder, as an enormous yacht passed beneath.

On the deck, two coltish looking young women in spaghetti-strap tank tops and waterfalls of bright blonde hair stared at the paused traffic.

"Is this how the other half lives?" Lena asked me as she surveyed the yacht and the rows of gleaming white apartment buildings and vacation homes that sprung up on the far side of the causeway.

"I think," I said slowly. "That it's how the other half of the other half lives."

She nodded. We'd tuned the radio to a local pop station and the new Zara Larsson single bopped out of the speakers. I drummed my fingers in time on the steering wheel.

Lena gave me a quizzical look.

"What?" I asked.

"This music isn't like you at all," she said.

"Music this poppy," I told her, "is appropriate to the locale. It's perfect beach music. I'm not so snobby that I can't appreciate a well-put-together pop tune."

"I thought you only liked music sung by skinny white guys moaning about how miserable they are," she said.

"I do," I said. "That, and tunes sung by Scandinavian women."

"You're such a guy," she said, making a face as she punched me in the arm.

We drove over the causeway and into the middle of St. Armand's Circle.

The haze that had greeted us on our arrival had lifted and the sky was nearly the same shade of blinding blue as the waters of the gulf.

On my driver's side window, I saw dolphins break water and hurriedly pointed them out to Lena, whose eyes widened in wonder.

"Amazing," she said, smiling and shaking her head.

We drove on under a lemonade yellow sun and into St. Armand's Circle.

The circle was a series of three roundabouts, each joined by a brief straightaway of street.

On each side of the circle, were long rows of shops. Each building was designed in the Spanish Mission style and was whitewashed against the sun.

Lena and I drove the full circuit of the key along a road pretentiously named the Boulevard of the Presidents, which terminated, at its southern end, at the South Lido Park and Nature Center.

Over a stand of dunes, I could see the Gulf of Mexico stretching implacably into the distance. We drove back to the beginning of the circle.

At the corner of Ringling Boulevard and South Adams Drive, I nosed the car into a space in front of a Starbucks and threw it into park. Lena turned in her seat and took off her glasses.

"Promise me you'll be careful," she said. "Always," I told her.

She turned her head and looked at the parade of fashionable shoppers outside the car window.

"I don't think I can compete," she said.

"You can," I told her. "Just think, you could be that lot over there."

I jerked my head in the direction of a family of tourists, just as fresh off the plane as we were, but nowhere near as rested.

A weary Dad and his equally tired-looking wife tried to ride herd over two well-fed children, who dragged each of them by the hand.

"Good point," Lena said. She gathered some stuff into her purse.

"I'll call you when I'm done," I told her.

"What time do you think that will be?" she asked.

"Hopefully, no later than one o'clock," I said. "I'm going to drive down to Siesta Key, have a look around, maybe ask some questions. I'll be back before you know it."

Lena leaned across her seat and kissed me, full on the mouth, and with surprising force.

"Call me," she said. "I will," I told her.

"I love you, Sean," she said, with what I thought was a note of sadness in her voice.

"You all right?" I asked.

"Sure," she said quickly. "I'm just going to worry about you, that's all."

"I'll be fine," I told her. "I'll be back soon."

"OK," she said, kissing me again before she climbed out of the car. "I'll see you soon."

She slammed the door behind her. And I waved to her through the glass as she melted into the line of shoppers.

I sat for a moment before I started the car again, pulled it into traffic and headed back across John Ringling Boulevard toward Siesta Key.

I fiddled with the radio as I drove back across the causeway and into downtown Sarasota. I let the stations cycle through twice before settling on a classic rock station.

"The waaaiiittingggg is the hardest part," Tom Petty warbled through the speakers at me.

"You have no idea, Tom," I told the radio as I drove south along U.S. Route 41 toward Siesta Key.

As I drove past a well-manicured garden, the Bogie and Bacall stateliness of old Florida that was downtown Sarasota collided sharply with the new Florida of the go-go, twenty-first century.

Here, the highway was a four-lane morass of steroid-driven retail development, buffet restaurants, nail salons, auto parts stores, and chain hotels.

Spaced at intervals of about four blocks were major inter-
sections allowing access to the big-box stores that some
builder had been thoughtful enough to slather with a thick
coat of tropical cutesy that just about concealed the industrial
brutality of the store beneath.

The parking lots, even at mid-morning on a weekday, were
packed.

And, in front of me, the barely visible heads of retirees
poked above the drivers' seats of Toyotas, Nissans, Chevys,
and Fords that were finished in the same blinding shade of
white.

Siri led me down this sterling example of the retail-indus-
trial complex for about six miles before I turned right onto
Siesta Drive, which connected the mainland to Siesta Key.

The view coming across Siesta Drive was much the same
as the one at St. Armand's Circle.

On each side of me, the Gulf of Mexico, impossibly blue and
lovely, slapped at the private docks of improbably large
homes.

I followed Siesta Drive down a road called Higel Avenue to
Midnight Pass Road, which dumped me into the middle of Siesta Key.

I took a left onto Beach Road and followed it for about three
or four blocks past a series of shops selling beach and surf
supplies until I came to an intersection with a street called
Calle Miramar.

On Calle Miramar, I made a quick left into a parking lot,
where I found a spot facing across the street.

It gave me a perfect view of a low, wood-paneled office building whose front was dominated by a large picture window that
had the words "Sunshine Properties" stenciled onto it in large
letters.

I sat for a moment, trying to figure out my next move. I
wasn't a detective.

I wasn't a cop. I couldn't just barge in there, shout "A-ha,"
in a deep, authoritative voice, and hope that whoever I found
there would be so impressed that they'd immediately explain

the links to a Pennsylvania state senator and a non-profit out-side Philly.

On the other hand, that kind of thing happened all the time on "CSI: Miami," so it wasn't entirely out of the realm of pos-sibility.

I lacked David Caruso's scene-chewing charisma, so that left me short of options.

Instead, I got out of the car, jammed on my trusty Harris-burg Senators baseball cap, donned a pair of sunglasses, grabbed a notebook and a pen, and trotted jauntily, I hoped – across the street to the front door.

CHAPTER 26

The top half of the front door to Sunshine Properties was framed in pebbled glass and the company's name was stenciled in gold letters on the front. A massive picture window, papered with advertisements for local rental properties, took up most of the rest of the building's frontage.

A tropical wind blew in from the ocean. And I could hear the steady and low hum of the air-conditioner inside the office. As I entered, I saw a Formica counter, about waist-high, running the length of the office.

Three Latina women sat at cluttered desks behind the partition, part of which swung up- ward at its far end to allow entrance to the formal office area.

A battered radio perched on top of some equally battered filing cabinets played salsa music. And one of the women, who was heavyset and wore her lustrous black hair in a tight bun, looked up as I entered.

"Can I help you?" she asked, regarding me skeptically over the top of a pair of half-glasses. Her brown eyes were not unfriendly, but neither were they particularly welcoming.

The two younger women, who sat in the rear of the room at desks that faced each other, remained silent and did not look up.

"I'm Sean Flynn," I said, mustering up about as much gravitas as I could. "I'm a reporter for a newspaper in Pennsylvania, and I'm working on a story. And I was wondering if I could ask you a couple of questions."

The older woman rose from behind her desk and walked to the counter. Her heels clicked rhythmically on the tiled floor.

"You have identification?" she asked.

I dug into my pocket for my wallet and fished out a business card from the morass of ATM withdrawal slips and meal receipts that I still needed to file for my monthly expense reports.

The older woman picked up the card without enthusiasm and held it as if I were a cat who had just dropped a dead mouse at her feet.

"And what do you want to know, Mr. Flynn?" the woman asked.

I shrugged.

"Your name, for starters," I said. "You have me at a disadvantage. I know your name, but I don't know yours."

The woman gave half a smile.

"Lourdes Santiago," she said, extending her hand. I took it, and we shook hands.

"Nice to meet you, Ms. Santiago," I said.

"That's 'Mrs. Santiago,'" she corrected me. "I have been married for 36 years."

"My apologies, and my congratulations," I told her. "You don't look like a lady who's been married for that long."

"You flatter me, sir," she said.

"Thanks, I try."

Behind her, the two younger women laughed.

"So how can I help you, Mr. Flynn?" she asked again.

I took my notebook out of my back pocket, flipped it to an open page, and slapped it onto the counter in front of me.

"Sorry," I said. "First off, can you tell me what sort of business this is?"

"Are you using my name?" Lourdes Santiago asked. Smart. She'd either read enough about reporters or seen enough on TV to know whether to ask if I was going to use her name.

"Not right now," I said. "I'm just gathering information."

She nodded, looked at my business card again, and looked at me.

"As you can probably tell from the name, we deal in real estate. Mostly they are rental properties for the area's Hispanic population. It's one of the largest and fastest-growing in the country."

I detected a note of pride in her voice. I scribbled down what she told me.

"And how long has this business been open?" I asked.

"For ten years," she told me. "We opened in 2008 after our employer, Oscar Veracruz, moved here from West Palm Beach. He's a member of the Hispanic Chamber of Commerce and a very well-respected businessman."

"I see," I said. "And can you tell me why a company in southwest Florida might be donating thousands of dollars to a tiny non-profit agency in suburban Philadelphia called The Greater Doylestown Development Corporation?"

"I have no idea," she said. "You would have to ask Mr. Veracruz about that. I know he has many interests."

Behind Lourdes Santiago, the two younger women were making a great show of not paying attention to our conversation.

The one on my left busied herself with some paperwork. Her colleague on the other side of the adjoining desks peered at a computer screen and tapped some keys.

Both had stiffened noticeably when I asked about the donations to Rocco Giambone's pet non-profit agency.

"Is Mr. Veracruz here now?" I asked.

Lourdes Santiago shook her head vigorously.

"Mr. Veracruz is out of the office all morning for business meetings, and then has a full slate of appointments this afternoon," she said. "If you like, I can make an appointment for you to see him."

"I'd like that very much," I told her.

Lourdes Santiago walked back to her desk and grabbed an appointment calendar. She returned to the counter, flipped a few pages and looked up at me.

"Is tomorrow at two o'clock, all right?" she asked.

"That'd be fine," I told her.

"Until tomorrow, then, Mr. Flynn," she said, extending her hand.

We shook hands again.

"Until tomorrow, Mrs. Santiago," I said.

We stared at each other for a moment and I saw ... something ... fear ... cloud her eyes for just a moment.

As I left, I cast one last glance at the two younger women. One of them held my gaze with something that looked like a plea.

Or it could have been a warning.

CHAPTER 27

The next day, I was back at Sunshine Properties at two o'clock on the dot.

Lourdes Santiago gave me a look filled with pity as I materialized at her front counter.

"Mr. ... Flynn, no?" she asked.

I nodded and smiled my winningest smile.

"How nice, you remember," I said.

"Hard to forget," Lourdes Santiago said curtly. "Right this way, please. Mr. Veracruz is waiting for you."

She flipped open the divider that led into the office space. The clerk on my left, the one I'd seen the day before, was still there.

A different woman, but with the same deep almond eyes as her colleague's, sat across from her.

The young woman from the day before glanced up as I passed, and our eyes met again.

Remembering the look she had given me during our last meeting, I had come prepared.

As I passed, I dropped a business card with my name and phone number onto her desk.

Lourdes Santiago had her back to me as she led me into Veracruz's office at the rear of the building. I hoped she didn't notice the drop.

Oscar Veracruz's office was at the end of a short hallway that terminated with two, identical particleboard doors. One of them led into a cramped washroom.

Through the half-open door, I saw cleaning solvents stacked beneath the sink.

The bathroom gave off a foul, chemical smell.

Veracruz was seated behind a bare desk that looked like one of those cheap, you-assemble-it jobs that you'd pick up at Target or Costco. He was seated when I arrived, staring at nothing. He rose as I entered.

"Mr. Flynn," he said, extending his hand across the desk. "I am Oscar Veracruz. How nice to meet you."

Veracruz's palm was limp and cold in mine. I squeezed, hard, and his eyes widened in surprise. Then, he smiled, displaying two rows of very white, very even, and very small teeth.

Veracruz looked to be somewhere north of forty years old.

But it was hard to tell. His dark skin was stretched, taut and even, over his face.

The only sign of age, or of character for that matter, were crow's feet at the corners of his very dark eyes.

His mustache and beard were neatly trimmed and salted through with gray.

Veracruz sat down, and the guayabera shirt he wore rippled in a faint breeze coming through his office window. He wore slip-on shoes and linen pants.

I settled into an office chair across from him and took out my notebook.

Veracruz leaned back in his chair and tented his hands on his chest. His chest rose and fell evenly. He didn't look worried. He didn't look excited. He didn't look much of anything at all.

"You are a journalist," he said in the same faintly accented English as Lourdes Santiago.

"I am," I said.

"It must be a very interesting line of work," he said. "Puts you in contact with all sorts of different people."

"It does," I told him with a faint smile. "It beats actually working for a living."

"Indeed," Veracruz said. "Well, if we could get started. I am very busy today, Mr. Flynn."

"Please, call me Sean," I said.

"Sean," he said. "And you may call me Oscar."

I nodded.

"Mrs. Santiago said you had been in business for ... what ... ten years," I asked, flipping a page in my notebook. "And that you moved here from West Palm Beach."

"That is correct," he said.

"And, your accent, I can't quite place it," I said.

"I am Cuban," Veracruz said. "My family was lucky to escape Castro. And I grew up in Little Havana in Miami."

I nodded and scribbled and said nothing. Sometimes, that's the best interview tactic.

Many people get uncomfortable with silence and they rush to fill it up. Sometimes, that leads them to say more than they intend.

Oscar Veracruz was not one of those people. He sat quietly while I wrote, waiting for the next question.

"Mrs. Santiago also tells me that you're very active in the community," I said. "Do you feel an obligation, as a successful businessman, to give back?"

Veracruz nodded vigorously, responding to the ego stroke.

"When we came here, my family and I had nothing – nada – Mr. Flynn," he said. "Our relatives in Little Havana took us in, gave us food, and helped set up my father in a county job. He worked like a dog, twelve, thirteen, fourteen hours a day, picking up garbage after rich people in Coral Gables."

He continued, smiling with satisfaction, looking at the small office around him.

"Now," he said. "I own rental properties in Sarasota, in Venice, in Northport, and in Wellington and West Palm Beach. This office may not look it, but I am a successful man. I have a beautiful wife, two beautiful children, and my mother and father have their own home in Miami with orange trees out back.

"I am successful, Sean," he concluded. "And because of that, I feel I must help those who came after me."

I nodded and continued writing. Without looking up, I asked, "So why would you be interested in a non-profit in suburban Philadelphia?"

"Ah, yes, my good friend Senator McGeehan," he said. "That is easily explained."

"Go ahead," I said, glancing up from my notebook and fixing Veracruz with a skeptical grin.

Veracruz's shark-like smile remained fixed in place, but it looked a little more strained now. And the friendliness was gone from his eyes, replaced by a look that might have been hostility. And I wasn't even pressing him that hard.

Clearly, he wasn't used to being questioned about much.

He shrugged, his arms extended and his palms facing up.

"There is not much to tell, I am afraid," he said. "As a leader of my community, I am active in Democratic politics. And your Senator McGeehan was here a few years ago for a fund-raiser at a home on Longboat Key. We got to talking, and I asked how I could help ... and one thing led to another."

His voice trailed off and he smiled enigmatically at me.

"And you decided that the best way to help your community was to start fire-hosing money onto a non-profit run by a union boss who employs professional leg-breakers, right?" I asked.

"I'm sure I don't know what you're talking about," he said.

I felt anger rise in my throat.

"Mr. Veracruz," I said. "Last year, a young man who worked for Senator McGeehan was killed. I don't know why, or by whom, but the more I keep asking about it, the more people seem like they don't want me to find out. And they've put me in the hospital to keep me from looking. They haven't been shy about it. I think you know exactly what's going on here."

Veracruz stared at me, hard, and rose from his desk. Leaning across it, he jabbed his extended index finger in the air at me.

"Mr. Flynn, because you are young, and therefore, stupid, let me spell a few things out for you," Veracruz said, his voice rising, even as his accent started slipping.

"Pennsylvania is filling with Hispanics," he said. If I help them, maybe get them a job, or help with immigration – especially in these challenging times -- maybe they'll have a better life. And, maybe, when the time comes, they'll remember who helped them."

He sat back in his chair and stared daggers at me.

"And that'd be you," I said.

"That is the way the world works," Veracruz said, his voice flat and filled with unmistakable menace. "I think you can find your own way out."

I did.

I passed Lourdes Santiago in the narrow hallway outside Veracruz's office. She looked at me, sadly, and then shook her head.

"It sounds as if things did not go well between you," she said.

"No," I said. "They didn't."

CHAPTER 28

That night, Lena and I had dinner at a white-tablecloth Cuban restaurant on Saint Armand's Circle.

The night was warm and breezy, and we sat under an awning and watched the tourists and locals walk by. The locals were easy to spot – they were the ones in the designer clothes and permanent tans.

So, too, for that matter, were the tourists.

They were sun- burnt and considerably less well-dressed. Granted, we were tourists too, but I liked to think that Lena and I had much better fashion sense.

She was wearing a cream white halter dress, and her thick hair was tied back.

Her green eyes shone in the gathering dusk and a tennis bracelet, studded with diamonds, gleamed on her pale wrist.

We were drinking daiquiris made in the classic way – none of that frozen slush.

I was wearing a white linen shirt and was trying very hard not to spill my drink on it. I had left two buttons open at the throat in the hope that it made me look rakish.

We were working on a small casserole of shrimp and crabmeat.

The casserole was topped with a thin crust of Romano cheese and was laced with artichoke hearts.

"This guy Veracruz sounds like bad news," Lena said, as she shoveled a bit more of the casserole onto her plate. There were many things I liked about her, but one of them was the Midwestern sensibility that she brought to the dinner table.

"He is," I said, trying to keep up with her. "And he's responded just like everyone else I've tried to talk to on this story – the more I ask, the more people seem to not want me to find anything."

"What are you going to do?" Lena asked as juice from the casserole dripped from the corner of her mouth. I took my napkin and reached across the table and wiped it off.

"Thank you," she said.

"You're welcome," I told her, taking a long pull from my drink and signaling the waiter for a refill.

"I'm going to do what I always do," I continued. "I'm going to keep nosing around, and hopefully do it in a way that doesn't land me in the emergency room again."

Lena's eyes softened as she stretched her hand across the table. I covered it with mine.

"I'm worried about you, Sean," she said.

I waved her off.

"Please don't be," I said.

"I know what you're going to say," I continued. "You're going to say that you care about me and can't help but worry. And I know that, and I love you for it. But I'm worried enough about myself. In seventeen years as a reporter, this is about the most dangerous thing I've ever gotten involved in. But if I know you're worrying, too, it's gonna make it that much harder to do the job. I can't be paralyzed by worry. It'll just be a distraction."

She smiled sadly and shook her head.

"I'm going to worry about you anyway," she said, her voice barely a whisper. There were tears in her eyes.

Our waiter picked that moment to arrive with our food, and Lena hurriedly dabbed at her eyes.

Somehow, she managed to not wreck her eye makeup as she did it.

The waiter put a plate of ropa vieja – shredded steak simmered with mixed vegetables and onion, served with rice – in front of me.

Lena had opted for mahi-mahi that had been marinated in citrus juice. It was served with rice and yuca.

"What are you going to do?" Lena asked me as she cut into her fish.

"Probably go back to Sunshine Properties and just watch the place for a while," I said. "I want to see who goes in and who comes out. And, hopefully, I'll get a call from the young woman I gave my business card to. She looked like she had something she wanted to tell me."

"Have you spoken with Marty Herman lately?" she asked. "No, but he's next on my list of people to call," I said. "We've been here a few days. That should have been more than enough time for him to poke around."

She nodded, and we finished our dinner in a silence that was only broken when Lena had cleaned her plate and began regaling me with tales of her shopping adventures.

After dinner, we walked hand-in-hand among the tourists and stopped to get an ice cream cone at a garishly decorated ice cream joint that was packed to the rafters with kitschy, 1950s bric-a-brac.

We kept walking through the warm night. Lena rested her head on my shoulder, and we followed the sound of the crashing surf to the entrance to Lido Beach.

We took off our shoes and walked on the sand to the edge of the water.

Lena sat down, smoothing her dress beneath her. She loosened her hair and it blew gently in the breeze.

I sat down beside her, resting my arms on my knees. We were both quiet, looking out at the surf of the Gulf of Mexico.

"Sean?" she asked finally. "Yeah, Lena?"

She turned to me, a plea in her eyes.

"You can play detective all you want tomorrow -- but tonight -- give me tonight," she said.

I leaned in to kiss her.

The decision wasn't hard to make.

CHAPTER 29

The next morning, I was parked across the street from Sunshine Properties and staring at the front door.

I had a paper take-out cup filled with coffee, two blueberry-cake donuts in a wax paper bag on the front seat, and absolutely no idea what I was looking for.

All in all, it wasn't different from most days. But my most days rarely involved trying to figure out a link between a Pennsylvania politician, a tough-guy union boss, and a southwest Florida slumlord.

I was listening to sports-talk radio, and the host was all a-twitter over some early season trading action for Tampa's pro hockey team.

I suppose it was important enough. But I've always believed that hockey has no business being played below the Mason-Dixon.

I turned off the chatter and turned on the Bluetooth. I opened Spotify, and a few seconds later, the opening chords of The Creation's "Biff Bang Pow" thundered out of the Passat's speakers.

Much better.

Twenty minutes later, I was still staring at nothing and debating whether to eat the second blueberry-cake donut when my cell phone rang. I answered it.

"Flynn," I said.

"Mr. Flynn?" a woman's voice asked. "Yes?" I said. "This is Sean Flynn."

"My name is Guadalupe Guerra," the woman said. "You gave me your business card yesterday."

I sat up in my seat and turned off the radio. I grabbed a notebook from my satchel in the backseat and furiously flipped it to a blank page.

"Of course, Ms. Guerra, thank you so much for calling," I said. "What's on your mind today?"

There was a pause. In the background, I could hear traffic noises. Was she outside?

"I want to talk to you, Mr. Flynn," Guadalupe Guerra said. "But not on the phone."

"OK," I said. "Where shall we meet?"

"There is a little café I know of," she said. "It's quiet and we will not be disturbed there."

Guadalupe Guerra gave me directions. When she was done, I put the car into drive and headed for downtown Sarasota.

The drive-in mid-morning traffic from Siesta Key to downtown Sarasota took about 25 minutes.

I parked the car on a quiet street behind Main Street and walked into a small café called El Pequeno Loro – the "little parrot."

Inside the café, the lights were low, and the walls were painted a subdued shade of burnt orange. Dark wood abounded and Guadalupe Guerra sat at a table at the back.

She nodded to me as I entered.

"Ms. Guerra," I said, taking a seat across from her.

"Mr. Flynn," she said.

We shook hands.

Her dark hair fell thick and lustrous over tanned shoulders and stirred gently in the breeze from one of the two ceiling fans that whirred noiselessly above our heads.

Guadalupe Guerra ordered coffee for both of us. I dumped in sugar and cream so that I'd have something to do with my hands.

Guadalupe Guerra watched me without saying anything. When I was done fiddling with the coffee, she smiled placidly -- and maybe a little sadly -- at me.

I took a sip of the coffee and arranged my notebook and pen on the table.

"Thank you for calling me," I said.

"You're welcome," she said. "But we haven't much time." "What do you mean?" I asked her.

A worried look furrowed her brow.

"My boss, Mr. Veracruz, is a very bad man," she said. "Whatever you are looking into, you must stop. No good can come of it."

"What do you mean?" I asked.

She looked around as if someone might be listening.

"When you came into the rental office the other day, what did you see?" she asked me.

"Not much," I said. "For someone as successful as your boss, it was a pretty shoddy operation. The office was a mess. It was sparsely furnished. And the paint was peeling."

She nodded, half-smiling.

"You are very observant," she said. "There's a reason for that. The rental office is a front."

My eyes widened.

"So what kind of business is Mr. Veracruz actually in?" I asked.

She cast her eyes down.

"Sometimes it helps to look like Jessica Alba," she said. "Sometimes it doesn't."

I leaned back in my chair and put one palm on my forehead.

"He's pimping you," I said. It wasn't a question.

All traces of humor vanished from Guadalupe Guerra's face and her full lips thinned to a tight, bloodless line.

"He came to my village in El Salvador," she said. "He said we'd be working as hostesses in his restaurants in Florida and that he'd help us get green cards."

I nodded, scribbling notes in my notebook.

"Don't tell me, let me guess, there was a small fee involved," I said.

She nodded.

"How much," I asked.

"Ten thousand dollars," she said. "He said he'd take it out of our pay, and that we would pay him back over time."

I nodded.

"And, of course, 'hostess' took on an entirely new meaning once you got here," I said.

She nodded and there were tears in her eyes.

"I haven't told my family," she said, looking away from me. "I can't. I just send back money when I can. They can't ever know what I'm doing."

"Why?" I asked. "They might be able to help you."

She shook her head, emphatically, her voice filling up the space between us.

"When I got here, I was living in Wellington, on the East Coast, and a brother of one of the young women showed up. He confronted Mr. Veracruz; said he was taking her back home to El Salvador."

I felt my throat tighten, and my grip close around my coffee cup. Anger, like a storm, rose in my throat.

"The boy was screaming at Mr. Veracruz," Guadalupe continued. "And Mr. Veracruz just laughed at him. He went outside with the boy and said he would explain everything. We heard a gunshot and Mr. Guerra came back into the house alone."

Across the table from me, Guadalupe Guerra looked very small, very alone, and very far from home.

"He said the same thing would happen to anyone who tried to take us away," she said, the tears flowing freely down her cheeks. Her shoulders shook with quiet sobs.

"Mr. Flynn – Sean," she said. "You seem like you are a good man. Please, whatever you are doing. Stop it now. Stop it before you get yourself killed."

She was right.

But I knew I wouldn't.

"I'm going to get you out of this," I told her.

CHAPTER 30

I was having lunch in the hotel restaurant and thinking things over when my cell phone rang.

"Flynn," I said.

"Sean. It's Marty," Marty Herman said. I could hear the buzzing of the Harrisburg PD's squad-room in the background. "I think I've got something."

I swallowed down the Cuban sandwich I was eating and chased it with a splash of iced tea. I reached to the floor to my satchel and pulled out a notebook and a pen.

"Whaddya got?" I asked.

Marty Herman grunted.

"Took me all freaking night, but I finally figured out how to work the Legislature's Web page," he said. "Once I found the damned bill, I had to translate it from legalese into English so I could figure out what it meant."

"I've been here nearly three days, Marty," I said, stifling a laugh. "It took you this long to get around to it? I'm starting to not feel like a priority in your life."

"I don't know if you've noticed, Flynn, but as a fully sworn law enforcement officer, I am often busy stopping bad guys, and working to keep the community safe for the citizens," he said.

"You couldn't figure out how to do it, could you?" I said.

"Not for the fucking life of me," Herman said. "I had to get one of the rookies fresh out of the academy to show me. Most goddamned embarrassing thing I've had to do in my life."

"The most?" I asked.

There was silence.

"Pretty damned near," Marty said. "But there was this one time when ..."

I cut him off.

"Back on task, Marty," I said. "You can tell me later. And we'll have to see about dragging you into the twenty-first century when I get back."

"All right, all right," Marty said. "Pushy bastard, aren't you?"

"It's one of the reasons you like me," I said.

"No, it's not," he said. "Anyway, I read through the bill, and, as near as I can figure, the bill provides a tax exemption for the development of a tract of land in Solebury Township in Bucks County."

"And who's developing the land?" I asked.

"Good question," Marty said. "And I knew you would ask that. I called one of my brother officers on the Solebury Police Department and had him check for me."

"Enterprising of you," I said.

"I am an investigator," Marty said. "I just follow the clues."

"And what's the name of the development company?" I asked.

"An outfit called Independence Partners," Marty said. "And that's about as far as I got. There was a double-fatal up on Allison Hill last night, and I was up there until God-Knows-When working the scene."

I hastily scribbled some notes.

"Great work, Marty," I told him.

"Glad you think so," he said. "Sorry I couldn't get more."

I waved a hand in the air, as I cradled the phone against my ear.

"No problem," I said. "I can chase down the corporate information myself. It shouldn't take too long."

"OK," Marty said. "What have you been up to down there?" I told him. When I was done, he let out a long, low whistle. "You've been busy," he said.

"I do try," I told him. I signaled the waitress for the check.

"Sean, can I ask you something?" Marty said. "Sure," I said.

"Have you noticed that the more you poke into this thing, the more people seem to threaten to break your legs?" Marty observed.

"It is a disturbing pattern," I told him. "And Lena is getting a little worried about the whole business."

I could hear Marty Herman chewing on something.

"Lunch?" I asked.

He grunted in assent through a full mouth.

"Pastrami on rye from the Sandwich Factory on Second Street," he said, and I could picture him spraying crumbs over the front of his uniform blouse.

"You are as constant as the northern star," I told him.

"Yeah ... whatever," Marty said. "Look, I got some vacation time coming. And, even though you are a royal pain in the ass, I like you. How about I come down for a day or two, kind of follow around behind you, and stay on the lookout for miscreants?"

"You'd do that for me?" I asked.

"Don't flatter yourself," Marty said. "Mostly, I'm doing it for that lady-friend of yours. And Christ knows when a chucklehead like you will find another one like her."

"Why, Marty," I said. "That may be the nicest thing you've ever said to me."

"Yeah, yeah," Marty said. "Where do you want to meet?"

The waitress returned with my check.

"Well, based on my conversation with that young woman I told you about, it looks like I'm headed for West Palm Beach," I said.

"All right," Marty said. "I'll look into flights and try to get on the next one tomorrow. I'll give you a call when I get there."

"Marty?" I asked.

"Yeah?"

"Thanks," I said.

"Don't mention it," he said. "But Flynn?"

"Yeah?"

"I may need a favor from you someday," he said.

"Yeah," I said.

We hung up.

The waitress smiled at me as I left the hotel restaurant.

"Have a good day, sir," she said.

I smiled back.

"I'll certainly try," I said.

I walked across the hotel lobby to the business center and settled down in front of a computer.

In a moment, I had called up the Pennsylvania Department of State's Web page. I clicked through a few sub-menus and got to their corporate information page.

I entered "Independence Partners" in the search window, and the computer buzzed and hummed as the search engine went through its paces.

Back when I was starting out as a reporter in Connecticut in the early 1990s, you had to call a toll-free number at the Secretary of State's office and an actual human being had to look up the information for you.

Depending on the person, and their level of cooperation, sometimes they'd find what you were looking for, sometimes not.

If "sometimes not" happened, you had to schlep down to Hartford to look up the information yourself. That meant a day of work gone. But it also meant a lunch on the company.

Life is full of trade-offs.

The search window filled with data and my eyes widened.

"Oh, my stars and garters," I said, as I hit the 'print' button. I grabbed the results, folded them up and stuffed them into my satchel.

Then I went upstairs to find Lena and so we could start packing for West Palm Beach.

CHAPTER 31

The next morning, Lena and I were driving south along Interstate 75 on our way to West Palm Beach.

The concierge at the hotel had told us that the drive would take around five hours.

We woke before dawn, threw our stuff into our bags, checked out, and left just as the rest of Sarasota was settling in for breakfast.

At this early hour, it was still cool for air conditioning, but the air had a defiant humidity to it that had caused our clothes to wilt against our bodies as we loaded the car.

I was wearing an old U2 tour t-shirt that was fraying at the collar. But I refused to throw it away because it would have meant surrendering some part of myself that I wasn't ready to part with yet.

I was fine with growing old. It was aging that bothered me. The t-shirt was complimented by a pair of clean, close-fitting jeans and vintage Adidas sneakers.

I wasn't wearing any socks.

Lena was wearing a coral-colored t-shirt with cap sleeves that revealed well-toned arms that glowed from a freshly acquired tan.

She was in a pair of low-rise jeans and slip-on shoes. Her gold tennis bracelet glinted at her wrist. A quick glance was all it took to remind me of how lucky I was to have this amazing woman sitting next to me.

The air in southwest Florida smelled vaguely of decay, sex, and the sea. It was the same heady mix that I'd smelled since we'd arrived.

And underneath it, all was the suggestion that rain was never far away.

Lena had opened the windows, and she smiled into the rising sun, her hair whipping about her as the speedometer on the Volkswagen crawled steadily toward 80 MPH.

Two take-out cups from Starbucks sat in the well between the bucket seats, and Lena dug bagels out of a paper bag.

The Florida air mixed with the burnt aroma of the mega-chain's coffee.

We headed south down I-75 past Nokomis and Venice and into the city of Punta Gorda, which was still recovering from a devastating hurricane that had blown through the state the year before.

From the highway, we could see the twisted skeletons of hotel signs that were bent in the middle and then twisted backward like they had been caught in the middle of some arthritic old man's stretching exercises.

Near a hotel with an empty pool was a roofless fast-food restaurant and the cinder-block remains of one of the count-less Waffle House restaurants that were a fixture of southern rest-stop life.

"Wow, Lena said, letting out a low whistle as we drove through the science-fiction landscape. "I'd heard that Florida had been hit badly by hurricanes last year, but I've never seen the damage up close before."

She turned down the radio – we'd found the one decent al-bum-rock station in southwest Florida – as if out of respect to the funeral scene unfolding on either side of us.

"It's a pretty stark reminder that we're just visitors here," I told her, taking one hand off the wheel and folding it around hers. "I've covered a few of these over the years. You never really get used to it."

"It's so sad," she said. "There were people who lost every-thing."

"Yep, that's true," I said, letting go of her hand and reaching for the coffee between us. I took a sip and put the cup back into its resting place. "But you know what every single person told me as they were cleaning up the wreckage that nature had left behind it?"

"What?" she asked.

"That they were lucky to be alive. That no one had been hurt," I said. "They said you could always replace stuff. But that it was impossible to replace a life."

Lena nodded.

"But that's what you expect someone to say when they're in shock, isn't it?" she asked.

I shrugged.

"It doesn't make it any less true," I said.

We drove on in silence for a while, letting the radio fill in the space between us as we raced south.

After about two hours on the road, we reached Fort Meyers and took what amounted to a sharp left onto State Route 80. This was a flat, featureless run that would take us all the way across the backbone of the state until we hit Wellington and West Palm Beach on the east coast.

We passed through towns named LaBelle, Harlem, and Clewiston until we hit Lake Okeechobee in pretty much the dead center of the state.

This run struck me as the old Florida.

Here, the orange groves had yet to be plowed under to make way for big-box development and the homes lacked the auto-CAD perfection of the faceless, gated developments that had sprung up all over Sarasota and into unincorporated Manatee County to its north.

The air here was lightly perfumed with the smell of burning sugarcane.

And I may have been imagining things, but I could almost feel time slow down amid the wind-beaten cardboard bunga-lows and the barbecue joints with the hand-painted signs that lined either side of the highway.

This part of the state, it seemed, had not yet adopted the breakneck pace that had been imported from the north and slapped with a fresh coat of pastel-colored stucco to fit in with the local surroundings.

Near midday, we passed the Palm Beach County prison and turned right onto State Route 882 for the final push into West Palm Beach.

"What are you hoping to find here?" Lena asked me as we cruised down the highway. I had one hand on the steering wheel. The other bounced nervously on my knee.

"Hopefully, a connection that'll cement the link between Veracruz, Giambone, and McGeehan," I said. "Guadalupe, from Sunshine Properties, told me that Wellington was the first place she landed when her boss, Veracruz, brought her in from El Salvador."

Lena turned in her seat to face me. She took off her sunglasses and her blue-green eyes were serious.

"And I know that's where Veracruz turned out Guadalupe and other women to hook for him," I continued. "I've also been told -- and need to nail this down when I get there -- that Veracruz wasted a brother of one of the young women in the West Palm house when he showed up and tried to liberate his sister."

Lena was shaking her head.

"I can't believe there's a connection between Senator McGeehan and all this," she said, anger, frustration, and maybe hurt, crept into her voice. "He's one of the most respected members of the Pennsylvania Senate. He authored the law creating the state's health insurance program for kids. He's a fucking legend, Sean."

I nodded.

"He's also a man with a lot of power, Lena. And he hasn't had a serious election opponent in how long?"

"Thirty years," she answered automatically as if the knowledge came from the same deep reserve in her brain that also told her that it was cold in the winter and warm in the summer.

"Thirty years," I repeated. "And he's got power. And he's got wealth. And he's got an iron grip on the Senate. I've been a reporter for nearly twenty years as well, Lena. And if I know one thing, it's dangerous for one person to have that much clout for so long and to go unchallenged. People start getting weird ideas about themselves when they have that much influence. And it doesn't help when they're surrounded by people who are essentially paid to revere them."

"But he's done so much good, Sean," she said.

I put a hand on her thigh and rubbed it reassuringly.

"A man can be both, Lena," I said. "Sometimes he can even be that from minute to minute."

There were tears in Lena's eyes, and she looked as if she was on the verge of telling me something -- but had swallowed it back.

"Do you think McGeehan had something to do with Pete Andre's death?" she asked.

"Maybe not directly," I said. "But he had a role in causing it. And he might have a role in what happened in Guadalupe Guerra and those poor women from El Salvador that Oscar Veracruz exploited. And he probably had a part in the beating that landed me in the hospital all those months ago."

We hit the West Palm Beach city limits.

"And it ends here," I said.

CHAPTER 32

Marty Herman was waiting for us in the hotel lobby when we arrived. He was reading a well-creased copy of the Miami Herald that matched the wrinkled khaki pants and short-sleeved polo shirt he was wearing.

The sport shirt's three buttons were open at the neck, and thick tufts of chest hair peeked out from the gap of the tropical print fabric.

There was a paper cup full of coffee on the little table in front of him and the remains of some kind of baked good. I'd have bet a week's pay that it was a cruller.

As usual, Marty's brown hair was cut close to his head. And even in the air-conditioning, he was sweating. You can take the boy out of Central Pennsylvania ...

"Jeez, they let just anyone into this place?" I said in a loud voice as the lobby doors hissed closed behind Lena and me.

Marty Herman looked up, scowling, at the interruption of his tranquility. But he broke into a wide grin as he saw us approach. He rose from the chair, his arms extended, to bring Lena into his embrace.

"Lena, so good to see you," he said and kissed her on the cheek. "You didn't leave this guy in Sarasota?"

Lena smooched him back.

"Good to see you, too, Marty," she said. "And not a chance."

Marty Herman nodded at me, seriously.

"Flynn," he said.

"Herman," I said back.

Lena shook her head in wonder.

"Are you guys trying to out-macho each other?" she asked.

"It's not me, it's him," I protested, not entirely convincingly.

"It's him, not me," Marty said, also failing to convince Lena.

She laughed.

"Sean, honey, I'll check us in. You and Marty can catch up," Lena said, as she gave me a quick peck on the lips and then headed off to the reception desk.

The lobby of the chain hotel near the West Palm Airport was finished in white: white tiles were on the floor.

The walls were painted a white that was now trending toward nicotine-stained and the furniture was upholstered in white. The overall effect was Mafia Princess chic, but I'm sure someone must have found it stylish at some point.

Like the rest of this part of the state, it was going over to seedy in a way that suggested that it was comfortable with the change.

I settled into a chair across from Marty. The wall above his head was mirrored and my very tired reflection stared back at me.

"When did you get here?" I asked, running a hand through my tousled hair as I tried to prod the road fatigue from my bones.

"Last night around ten o'clock," Marty said. He leaned in to take a sip of coffee. When he frowned, I knew it had gone cold. Marty usually drank his coffee at a temperature set to rival the heart of the sun.

"Trip was all right?" I asked.

Marty made a face at the cup and put it back down on the table.

"Fine if you don't count the screaming kid ahead of me and behind me. They got screaming baby sections on planes now?"

"Ahhh ... Marty," I said. "Just shows you're not a parent."

"Yeah?" he asked. "And you base your wisdom on how many years of fatherhood? I'm still wondering why Lena hasn't dumped your ass yet."

"I'm touched by your concern, Marty," I said.

"Yeah, right," he shot back, and then changed the subject. "What's our first move?" he asked.

I nodded, looking around for, and then located the soda machine that buzzed temptingly in one corner of the lobby. Ahh ... for just a shot of caffeine right now. Just something to chase away the fatigue.

"First move is to check out Oscar Veracruz's property here in Wellington," I said. "We'll ... ahhh ... reconnoiter and then see where that leaves us."

Marty grinned.

"Reconnoiter," he said. "Nice. You've been watching Magnum repeats again?"

I ignored him.

"Least I didn't say 'surveil,'" I said.

Marty nodded emphatically.

"Hate that fucking word," he said. "So, while we're ahhh ... reconnoitering ... what are we looking for?" "Pretty simple," I said. "Any proof that the premises are being used as a house of ill-repute."

"You mean hookers, right?" Marty asked.

"And you wonder why you never made detective," I told him.

"Yeah, yeah," he shot back.

"My point exactly Officer Herman," I said.

"So, Sgt. Preston, when you do want to make your little trip?" he asked.

"Let me go upstairs and change, freshen up," I said. "We'll meet back here in thirty minutes."

I looked over at Lena, who was standing by the reception desk.

She mouthed the words "hot tub" to me and did a little dance as she dangled our room key in the air.

"Better make it forty-five," I told Marty Herman, who was already headed for the elevator.

Marty grabbed his newspaper and the chilled remains of his coffee.

"Maybe there's some college hoops on cable," he said as he headed for the elevator.

"Dare to dream," I told him as we walked.

I ended up being an hour late.

CHAPTER 33

Later, Marty and I were driving south along Forest Hill Boulevard into the heart of downtown Wellington.

The highway was the spiritual twin of U.S. Route 41 that cleaved through the middle of Sarasota.

Both sides of the four-lane highway were lined by brutal big-box development that had been painted in varying shades of coral pink and finished with hasty layers of Spanish tiles.

The palm trees that sat in the middle of meticulously planted islands looked like they'd been brought there as enemy combatants.

Once every three blocks, we came to a massive intersection that led into equally preposterous developments. Each looked the same.

Roughly 50 yards of driveway led to a set of massive gates with a guardhouse.

And as I looked at them, I couldn't be sure if they were intended to keep intruders out -- or were there to make sure the locals didn't leave.

Touristy northerners that we were, Marty and I gawked at the scenery.

"You see that?" he asked, pointing to a cluster of strip malls.

"The convenience store was bigger than my first house," I told him.

"Where you from, anyway, Flynn?" Marty asked.

I was driving. The radio was tuned to an album-rock station --- Marty's choice, not mine. Boston's "More than a Feeling" blared from the Passat's speakers.

It took every bit of will- power I had not to change the station.

"I was born on the western slope of the Rockies," I told him. "Grand Junction, Colorado. Moved to Connecticut early on.

But I haven't lived there in years. I guess I don't really feel like I'm from much of anywhere these days."

Marty nodded.

"I know the feeling," he said. "How long you been at The Banner?"

"Eight years," I told him. "Came here after my first marriage ended. I was living in California. And Harrisburg seemed about as far as you could get from Orange County without needing a passport. I sat down nearly a decade ago, and now, here I am."

"Yeah," Marty said, drumming the dashboard with one hand. "Here we are."

I glanced down at the scrap of paper balanced on my right knee. The address to the house we're looking for was written on it in Guadalupe Guerra's hesitant script.

She'd thrust the paper into my hand as I'd left our meeting at the café in Sarasota.

"Speaking of which, we're here," I said, as I steered the Passat into the driveway of still another oppressively large housing development.

"Oh goody," Marty Herman said.

The development looked just like the others. Two massive walls, each about 20 feet high, were finished in orange pastel and seemed to run for miles around the neighborhood's perimeter until they were bisected by a pair of huge, wrought iron gates.

On one of the walls, the name of the development, "The Olympiad," had been painted in Gothic letters almost as tall as the walls themselves.

"Jesus Christ," Marty Herman muttered under his breath as he took in the scene.

"Mhmhmm," I said as we pulled up to a gatehouse.

Inside the gatehouse sat a bored-looking old man in an ersatz cop uniform whose manner gave us the impression he was waiting for nothing so important as his next tee time.

"Can I help you?" he asked. The badge on his uniform blouse read "Stein." There were deep perspiration rings under his arms, and his breath smelled faintly of beer.

I smiled my winningest smile.

"Tom Rosencrantz," I said. "I'm here to see the Guilden-sterns."

Behind me, I heard Marty Herman stifle a laugh.

"The whoses?" the elderly guard asked.

"The Guildensterns," I repeated, hoping that such a family lived within.

The old security guard flipped through a directory.

"On Aphrodite Drive?" he asked.

"Yep," I said, grinning. "That's the one."

"Follow the access road and make your second left near the Clubhouse," the old guard said. "Aphrodite Drive is your third right just after the statue of Poseidon."

"Thanks," I said as the guard slid a visitor's pass under the windshield. There was every chance we'd been photographed as we came through the gate. But I noticed he didn't bother to ask for I.D., and I didn't see him take down our tag numbers.

We drove into the development. I ignored the directions the guard gave me and began looking for the address that Guada-lupe Guerra had given us.

Several wrong turns, and at least two passes by a huge pond with twin fountains in the middle of it, I pulled the Passat into a small street called Library of Alexandria Circle.

Next, to me, Marty Herman let out an exasperated sigh.

"'Library of Alexandria Circle?" he asked. "Are you kidding me?"

"Architect must have had a god complex," I said. "Or some-thing," Marty shot back.

I shrugged.

I threw the car into park at the far end of the street. We were looking for No. 54, so I assumed it was at the far end of the street.

No need to call attention to ourselves yet.

Library of Alexandria Circle wasn't much more than an al-ley that ran behind a larger street. On each side was a series of identical duplexes.

Each was painted white. And each had a heavy wooden door that was probably intended to look like the door to a

Spanish mission. And there were more of those goddamned tiles.

The design attempt failed. The duplexes had about much charm as a Taco Bell.

Each duplex had a small yard, not much more than five feet by about eight feet. The yards were covered by sharp, spiky blades of grass that looked like they'd cut your feet if you walked on them barefoot.

Number 54 Library of Alexandria Circle was about halfway down on the right-hand side. A monstrous Lexus sport-utility vehicle was parked out front.

The lawn had massive crop circles burned into it. I could only assume that the occupants kept a wolf as a pet.

I glanced to my right and noticed that Marty Herman was a loosely holding his service weapon in his right hand.

I jerked my head in the direction of the gun.

"You think we're gonna need that?"

"Hope not," he said gruffly. "But you can never tell about these things. I checked it through just in case."

We came up to the house. My nostrils twitched and my eyes burned. There was an acrid, chemical smell in the air around the house.

"What the hell is that?" I asked.

Marty shrugged.

"Search me," he said, then, abruptly, grabbed me by my forearm as I headed for the front door.

"Uh-uh," he said. "Stick with me."

I followed him around the right side of the house to a bank of low windows that looked out on the wall of the next duplex. We ducked low beneath the windows. From inside the house, I could hear hip-hop music.

Kneeling, we peeked in over the windowsill.

We were staring into a kitchen. In front of us, I could see a long, low granite countertop and cabinets finished in dark wood above.

I heard footfalls and dropped below the sill.

When the footfalls went quiet, Marty and I peeked in again to see two Latina women talking quickly to each other in Spanish.

The chemical smell was stronger now.

"You catch any of that?" Marty asked me in a hoarse whisper.

"Are you kidding me?" I answered. "I barely speak Spanish."

"Too bad," Marty said.

We heard another set of footfalls. The two young women were joined by a slightly older woman who was holding a young boy.

She had the same honeyed skin and her thick, dark hair was tied back tightly into a bun.

Like the two younger women, she wore the Floridian uniform of shorts, t-shirt, and open- toed sandals.

"They're cooking again," she told the other two. "I need you two to take the baby for a while until they're done."

Next, to me, I heard Marty draw a sharp intake of breath. When I looked at him, his jaw was set in a hard line and there was cold fury in his eyes.

"What?" I asked him.

He turned to me, staring hard, his breath coming in short, quick bursts.

"Those ladies are living in a meth lab, Sean," he said. "And they've got kids in there."

"What are we gonna do?" I asked him.

"We're going to stop it," Marty Herman said.

CHAPTER 34

My mouth fell open.

"A meth lab?" I repeated, even though I'd perfectly heard what he'd just said.

Marty nodded at me, his eyes cold and hard and serious.

"I've seen this stuff up on Allison Hill back home," he said. "Last year, we busted this place, up around Thirteenth and Berryhill, with some guys from the Attorney General's Office. I'll never forget the smell. There was shit everywhere. Kids were playing among the chemicals. The whole place was a tinder- box. If it went up, it would have taken half the block with it." "OK," I hissed under my breath. My palms were sweating.

And I could feel perspiration dripping down my back. "I'm all for little kids not getting roasted. But you got a plan on how you want to do this? Or do you just want to go storming in there like some Jewish Chuck Norris?"

Marty grinned at me.

"I've always said that my people could use an action hero," he said.

"Don't your people usually subcontract that out to the goyim?" I asked.

"You ever heard of the Six-Day War?" Marty said.

"Sure."

He smiled wickedly.

"I rest my case," he said.

"All right. All right," I said. "I'm on board with it. But how do you want to do this? We've only seen the women and children. There could be 30 guys in there, each of them armed with a blunderbuss, for all we know."

"Blunderbuss?" Marty asked.

"Uh-huh," I said. "A blunderbuss."

We had retreated to the car while we deliberated.

"You do have a point there," Marty said. "We could be kind of outnumbered."

"That's what I'm saying," I told him. "And wouldn't your brother officers here on the Wellington P.D. take exception to you barging into someone's domicile without a warrant?"

"But we do have probable cause," he said.

"OK," I said. "But how much do you value your pension?"

Marty thought it over.

"There's a clear and present danger," he said. "I saw it, and, as a sworn officer of the law, I did something about it."

"That's your story?" I asked.

"Yes," Marty said, he was looking up the street toward the house.

"Fair enough," I said. "Now what do we do about it?"

"First, I reconnoiter," Marty said. "Go see what we're up against. Gimme your keys?"

I handed him the keys, and Marty went around to the backseat, where he'd tossed a black duffel bag he'd brought with him from the hotel.

He unzipped it and took out a gun. He reached back into the bag, pulled out a spare clip, and tucked it in his pocket.

He checked the action on the gun, and then looked at me.

"Wait here," he said.

"You'll get no argument from me," I said, as I watched Marty jog back up the street toward the house again.

While he was gone, I leaned against the car and tried to look inconspicuous.

No sir, no one here except us Pennsylvanians about to execute an unconstitutional and illegal raid on a private residence.

Involuntarily, I began to whistle "If I Only Had a Brain," from the "Wizard of Oz."

I was about halfway through the third verse when Marty returned.

His face was red, and his forehead was covered in sweat. It was late afternoon, and the sun was starting to go down behind the palm trees at the far end of the development.

"So?" I asked him.

"All I can see are the women," he said. "I looked around the back of the house. There's a pool with one of those big screens over it that they seem to like so much around here. A pair of French doors led into the house. When I was back there, one of the doors was open."

Marty returned to the backseat, opened the door and fished something out of the black duffel. He handed me a snub-nosed .38 six-shooter.

I looked at it like he'd just handed me a dead fish.

Marty caught my expression and scowled.

"I take it you don't know how to use one of these," he said.

I nodded.

"For chrissakes, Marty, I'm a reporter," I said. "The last time I picked up a gun, I was 15, listening to The Police, and playing LazerTag."

Marty laughed.

"All right," he said.

He took the gun from me, loaded six bullets into the chamber, and gave me five more for my shirt pocket. He quickly showed me how to sight along the barrel.

"And remember, squeeze the trigger, don't pull it," he said. "The gun's going to jerk upward with the recoil, and you'll shoot above your target."

He showed me where the safety was and handed the .38 back to me.

"Feel better?" he asked.

"I feel like Phillip Marlowe with none of the cool," I told him.

He appraised me.

"Yeah," he said. "You look like it, too. Let's go."

I shoved the .38 into the front pocket of my jeans and prayed that I wouldn't have to use it. A thin line of sweat was running down my back, and my mouth felt like it was stuffed full of cotton.

We got to the heavy, oak-paneled front door. There was a slender, stained glass window running the length of the right side of the door. Just to the right of that was the doorbell, set into the pink stucco. Marty rang it.

A minute went by. Then another minute.

We heard footsteps and I drew a short intake of breath.

Beside me, Marty Herman was breathing evenly. His dark eyes were set on the door, and one hand was on the 9mm. that he'd brought with him from the car.

The door opened a crack and a beautiful, young Hispanic woman peered out.

Her eyes were filled with fright. She was no less lovely for it.

"Yes," she said in heavily accented English.

"Cable company," Marty said, trying to look friendly. "Routine visit. We're here to check your connections."

The young woman shook her head.

"We do not have ... cable," she said.

She began closing the door.

Marty looked at me frantically.

I jammed a foot in the door, and I grimaced as the heavy wood slammed against it.

"My name's Sean Flynn," I said through clenched teeth. "Guadalupe Guerra sent me."

She stopped pushing on the door. The crushing pain in my right foot began to subside.

"You know Guadalupe?" she asked.

"I do," I said. "I'm a journalist from Pennsylvania. I'm working on a story that may involve Oscar Veracruz. Can we come in? I'd like to ask you a few questions."

She smiled.

"I am Guadalupe's sister, Inez Guerra," she said, and there were tears in her eyes. "She is alive? She is okay?"

"She's fine," I said, and I smiled reassuringly. Marty Herman was glancing around nervously.

"May we come in?" he asked.

"Of course," Inez Guerra said. "But you cannot stay for very long."

She opened the door and we went inside.

CHAPTER 35

We stepped over the threshold and into a low foyer. The air was permeated with the smell of bleach, and somewhere, I could hear a baby crying.

To our right was a small sitting area, decorated with a cocktail table and two chairs. There were antique liquor prints in heavy frames on the wall. And above us, a ceiling fan whirled.

We followed Inez Guerra up a small flight of stairs that led into the kitchen that we'd seen through the window. A granite-topped counter with three stools separated the kitchen from a small living room.

There were two sets of doors off the living room – one on each side of the staircase that led to the second floor.

The wall to our immediate right was taken up by a pair of French doors that led to the pool outside. Through the door, I could see the pool, azure and still in the glow of the setting sun.

Inez Guerra's dark eyes were set deep in her face. And, like her sister, her coal-black hair spilled down her back.

She wore a tiny, brown and white flowered sun- dress. On her feet were a pair of sandals and her toenails were painted a shade of deep red.

"Do you have any things?" I asked.

"Not very much," she said. "Are you taking me to Guadalupe?"

"Yes," I said, casting a nervous eye around the room. Upstairs, I could hear the two women talking to each other in rapid-fire Spanish as the baby continued to cry.

"Take what you can, throw it in a bag, and let's get out of here," I told her. "You aren't safe here. This house is filled with dangerous chemicals."

Inez nodded.

"I know what they do here," she said, her face creasing with disgust. "I hate it. They make poison. And with a baby in the house."

Marty nodded.

"Sean, we gotta go," he said, urgently.

"I know," I hissed at him. "Inez, please, there's not much time. Get your things."

"Yes," she said, as she turned to leave. "But what about my friends? And the baby?"

I looked at her helplessly.

"I can only save so many people at one time," I told her. "When we get clear of here, we'll call the cops and child services. My friend is a police officer. They'll listen to him."

She nodded and left the room.

As we waited, Marty and I exchanged silent looks. We were thinking the same thing: What next?

Someplace in the house, a radio was on. I could hear Warren Zevon's "Lawyers, Guns, and Money." At least they had the vibe right. I snorted.

"What?" Marty asked.

"The song," I told him. "Zevon."

Marty chuckled.

"Yeah, I noticed that too," he said.

Upstairs, we heard footfalls and a sharp, quick volley of Spanish. When it was done, Inez Guerra reappeared carrying a small Louis Vuitton bag.

"You ready?" I asked.

"Yes," she said. "I told my friends, Ana and Marisol, that they should be ready to leave soon, too."

"Good job," Marty Herman said. "Let's get out of here."

As we made to leave, the heavy front door opened. Accompanied by two giant Latino guys in matching tracksuits who each looked bigger than the entire Florida State defensive line, Oscar Veracruz stepped across the threshold.

At first, he was surprised. Then his face hardened into contempt as he slowly recognized me.

"Amigos," he said. "To what do I owe this pleasure?" Behind me, I could hear Marty Herman shift the gun in his hand.

"We won't be staying," I said.

The two heavies advanced on us.

"Oh, but I think you will," Oscar Veracruz said.

As if by reflex, I could feel myself reaching for the gun in my pocket.

And I shoved Inez Guerra, hard, behind the kitchen counter.

The two heavies came at us, reaching beneath their sweat-suit tops, and there was a sharp pop as Marty Herman fired his gun.

The first shot hit the heavy to my right in the fore- head, leaving a small hole, and a look of complete shock, in its wake. He went down without a sound.

From the corner of my eye, I could see the other two young women, Ana and Marisol, crouching at the balcony that looked over the kitchen and living room.

"Get down and get out of here," I shouted to them.

They retreated to a back bedroom. As the second heavy advanced, I said a hurried prayer and squeezed off two rounds from the .38. I knew I probably wouldn't hit the broad side of a barn, but I was hoping for the best.

The first shot clipped the bruiser on the right arm. He grunted in pain. The second got him in the left leg, he cried out and went down. Blood was gushing from the wound.

The whole thing had taken less than 15 seconds, but it felt like an eternity.

I stared at the gun in my hand and put it down on the nearby kitchen counter. Inez Guerra emerged from behind the counter. Her eyes were wide with fear.

Marty Herman was already checking the wounded bruiser, even as he kept an alert watch on Oscar Veracruz, who wore an expression of defeat mixed with fury.

"You will pay for this," he said to both of us.

"Maybe," Marty Herman said, as he attended to the wounded bruiser. He took a tea towel that I handed to him and tied it around the wound.

Without looking away, Marty said, "We're going to leave. And you're not going to stop us. And after we're gone, you're going to call 911 and get some help for your friend here. Otherwise, he's going to bleed to death."

"Why should I let you leave?" Veracruz said.

I answered this time. Behind me, I could feel Inez Guerra clinging to my back.

"Because you don't have a choice," I said. "And because I know how you're reinvesting the profits from your little operation here."

Veracruz looked at us, expressionless.

"You're also going to let us go to Sarasota and fetch Guadalupe Guerra out of the hellhole you have her in. You're going to let us do the same with those two young women and the baby up-stairs. After we're gone, we'll leave you alone. You can stay in business here, or not. You're scum. But right now, all I care about is getting these women out of here," I said.

"And if I don't agree?" he asked.

I glanced back at Marty.

"Then my friend here, who takes a great aversion to the kind of operation you're running will – emphatically – convince you otherwise," I said.

Veracruz was maybe a head taller than Marty Herman. But Marty had him by probably 20 pounds and a lifetime of boxing.

Veracruz was evil, but he was also a businessman. He knew a deal when he saw one.

"Agreed," he said. Then he looked at me. "But I hope our paths never cross again."

"I don't think you'll have to worry about that," I told him. "If I do, I don't think I'll be nearly so flexible," Guerra said. "I know," I told him.

Veracruz smiled a feral smile. Some of his pride was returning. I could hear the two gunnies groaning.

"Oscar," I said. "I have one more question."

"You can ask, but I doubt I'll answer," he said.

"Why McGeehan?" I asked. "Why you'd launder your money through him?"

Oscar Veracruz grinned and shrugged, both palms outstretched.

"The oldest reasons in the book, amigo," he said. "He liked money. And he liked the women."

I swallowed back the disgust rising in my throat – along with the urge to knock Veracruz in his backside.

"What was his cut?" I asked.

"Ten percent," Veracruz said. "I was always impressed. He was never greedy. And I was looking forward to expanding to the north."

I shrugged, palms up.

"I guess you'll have to find another business opportunity," I said.

"Yes," Veracruz said. "They come along more often than you'd think."

"They do at that," I said. I looked at Marty Herman and then to Inez.

"We're leaving," I said.

I took Inez Guerra by the hand and led her past Veracruz. Their eyes met for a moment as we left. Inez Guerra's eyes flashed with anger and she spat on Veracruz, hitting him in the chest.

"Cabron," she said.

Veracruz was silent.

Marty Herman followed behind us, keeping the gun trained on Veracruz.

In the distance, we could hear sirens.

"Take care," he said, smiling genially like he'd just dropped off the day's milk.

The two young women, holding bags and the baby, rushed past us and into the street.

They ran down a gap between two houses and we lost them in the gathering darkness.

When we were back at the car, I reached into my pocket and pulled out my phone. It had been recording the whole time. I clicked it off and brandished it in the air at Marty Herman.

"What the hell is that?" he asked me.

"An insurance policy," I said. We all got into the rental car and hightailed it back to the hotel. The first squad cars were driving past us as we left.

CHAPTER 36

We made it back to the hotel in record time.

Marty Herman drove, fast, but not too fast, through the sleepy streets of Wellington. I sat beside him and glanced constantly into the rearview mirror, expecting cops to materialize at any time.

Inez Guerra sat quietly in the back seat. Her head resting on her knees.

She was quiet. The air was heavy, in fact, with stillness. I saw the beads of sweat on Marty Herman's forehead.

I could hear Inez Guerra's steady intake of breath, and, beneath it all, the staccato beating of my heart in my chest.

Before tonight, I'd been a different person. Before tonight, I'd never fired a gun, much less picked one up. Before tonight, I'd never trained to defend myself. I'd never felt the kind of anger welling up in me as I did when Veracruz's two leg-breakers had advanced on me.

I was tired, I think, of getting pushed around. Tired of watching the injustice I'd spent my entire adult life writing about me go unanswered, go unavenged.

Peter Andre was nearly seven months dead. And at least now I had an inkling why. He'd known too much. And maybe, just maybe, he'd confronted it, demanded that it stop. And it got him killed.

I'd already made up my mind. We'd return to Sarasota and get Guadalupe Guerra and reunite her with her sister. After that, we'd go home and I'd confront McGeehan, Keller, and Giambone with everything I knew and everything I thought I knew.

And after that, I'd do what I do best: Write about it. And maybe that would change things.

In the gathering darkness, I looked at my reflection in the rearview mirror. And for the first time in a long time, I really felt like my age.

Thirty-nine isn't old enough to be called old. But nor was I a young man anymore. There were the beginnings of crow's feet at the corner of my brown eyes.

And my forehead was a little higher than I remembered it.

My eyes looked haunted. And I wondered if I'd ever be able to get the sound of that gunshot out of my head.

Or the smell of gunpowder mixed with the metallic taste of fear in mouth and the sharp, coppery redness of the bruiser's blood.

Somewhere beneath all of that, I'd heard the baby cry, and that had made my decision all that much easier.

I started breathing – hard. And I rocked back and forth in my seat, hugging my arms to me.

"Sean," Marty Herman said quietly, not looking away from the road. "Are you all right?"

I didn't answer. I just shook my head and continued rocking back and forth. My breath was coming in ragged gasps and my eyes burned.

"Sean," Marty said again, more forcefully this time, taking a huge hand from the wheel and laying it on my shoulder. "Are you all right? Answer me, man."

I gasped and pulled myself upright, my eyes wild and wide, I turned and stared at the cop who'd been a source and was now my best friend.

"I shot someone tonight, Marty," I said.

Marty Herman nodded grimly.

"Yes," he said. "You did."

"I didn't have any choice," I said.

"No, I didn't," I said, looking at my hands and feeling a lot like Lady Macbeth in search of the nearest washroom.

Marty pulled the car to the side of the road, threw it into park and looked at me.

"This is going to suck – for a while," he told me. "And it'll haunt you in your dreams for a long time. But you have to remember one thing: he was going to kill you. And you didn't have any choice."

I stared at him.

"You didn't have any choice," Marty repeated, grabbing me

by both shoulders and looking me square in the eye.

"You've shot someone before, haven't you, Marty?" I asked. Marty Herman nodded.

"Does it get easier?" I asked.

"No," Marty said, "It doesn't. But you make your choices and you live with them. There are things in this world you can stop. There are things in this world you can change. And there are things you wished you'd stopped or things you wished you'd changed. I try to have as few of those as possible."

"How's that working out?" I asked.

Marty laughed without mirth.

"Not as well as I'd like," he said.

He pulled the car back into traffic and we drove in silence back to the hotel. In the backseat, Inez Guerra looked at both of us, a small smile on her lips.

Then she was quiet, too, staring out the window at the passing lights and the quiet exchange of commerce in the endless procession of strip malls.

When we got back to the hotel, Marty pulled up to the front door.

"You two get out," he instructed me, as he handed me the cardkey for his room. "Take this lady upstairs and bring her to Lena. You go to my room and I'll meet you there. I'm going to try to park the car someplace inconspicuous."

I nodded without saying anything and got out of the car. I went around to the back and opened the door for Inez Guerra, who extended one fawn-like leg, and then another, as she got out of the car.

I took her hand and brought her inside. Behind me, I could hear Marty pull the car away into the darkness.

We walked through the lobby without making eye contact with any of the other guests. The elevator was down a small hallway behind reception. I hit the button.

The elevator door opened and we stepped inside. I punched the button for the sixth floor and looked at Inez Guerra. She looked exhausted.

"I'm bringing you to my girlfriend, Lena," I told her. "She'll take care of you. Wash up, get some sleep We're gonna get out of here in the morning, so I can take you to your sister."

At that, Inez Guerra's eyes widened and brightened.

"Thank you," she said, smiling. "You're kind."

"I do my best," I said, not really feeling particularly great at all. I could still hear the gunshot echoing my ears and my arms jerking with the recoil of the gun.

They ached. And all I wanted to do was sleep.

The elevator doors opened, and I looked cautiously in each direction before I led Inez from the elevator. We took a left out of the elevator vestibule and headed down the softly carpeted hallway, our footfalls were absorbed by the soft pile of the rug.

About ten feet down, and on our left, I stopped before our door. I slid the cardkey in and heard the click as the lock gave way.

Lena was sitting on the edge of one of two queen-sized beds.

She was wearing jeans a tee-shirt, and her hair was pulled haphazardly into a ponytail.

She leaped from the bed when she saw me, rushed to me, and threw her arms around me.

"Sean!" she said, burying her head into my neck. We kissed quickly.

"Miss me?" I asked.

"I've been worried sick," she said. "What happened?" I told her everything – well, nearly everything. When I was done, her mouth was agape.

"You left Veracruz alive?" she asked, an edge to her voice that might have been fear or annoyance.

"I had to," I told her. "He's our insurance policy."

Lena jerked her head at Inez, who was standing behind me, leaning against the wall.

"And what do you want me to do with her?" Lena asked, an unaccustomed tension in her tone.

"Just look after her tonight," I said. "Don't answer the door for anyone. I'll call you in the morning before it's time to leave."

"All right," Lena said. She walked with me to the door.

We kissed at the threshold.

"This is all gonna be over soon," I told her. "I promise. And I love you."

Lena nodded. Her eyes were far away.

"I know it will be, Sean," she said. "I love you, too. I'll see you in the morning."

The door closed and I waited until I heard the lock click in the door before I left.

I went down the hall to the elevator and punched the button. Marty's room was two floors above. After a moment, I was joined by two other guests, a big guy with red hair and a skinny kid who looked like he could have been a surfer.

The red-haired guy smiled a little too widely at me, and I felt the hairs on the back of my neck go up. The surfer kid bounced back and forth on the balls of his feet; his hands clenched in front of him. They both smelled like tobacco.

"Evening," I said.

"Hey, dude," the surfer kid said.

The elevator doors opened, and as they did, I felt something heavy collide with the back of my head.

I saw stars.

Then my vision went black.

CHAPTER 37

The circle of assailants closed around me.

As he drew closer, I could see that the glinting thing in Hamhock's hands was a nine-millimeter. He cocked and stood over me.

"This isn't going to end well, is it?" I asked him, spitting blood from my mouth, and trying not to retch. My heart was pounding in my chest and my eyes burned with tears. But if this was the end, I didn't want to beg. I didn't want to whimper.

At least I hoped I wouldn't.

"Not for you," Hamhocks said. He pointed the barrel toward the center of my forehead. I resisted the urge to squeeze my eyes closed. I waited for the inevitable.

"Can I just ask you something?" I said.

Hamhocks looked to Surfer Kid and they exchanged wry grins.

Hamhocks jerked his head at me.

"He wants to ask me something," he said, laughing.

Surfer Dude laughed a dry, hoarse laugh that rattled his chest.

"Sure," Surfer Dude said. "Why not? It's not going to change how things end here tonight."

"You got one question, pal. And then it's over," Hamhocks said to me. "You understand?"

I nodded and spit out more blood.

"I just want to know why," I said.

"Waste of a question," he said, shaking his head, taking in surfer dude with his glance. "We don't do why. We just ... ahhh ... specialize in ... what would you call it, Jimbo?"

Surfer Dude – Jimbo --- chimed in: "Content-delivery," he said. "And logistics."

Hamhocks laughed.

"Yeah," he said. "We don't do why. We just do logistics."

I nodded.

"Fair enough," I said. Sweat pooled in my back. My shirt was soaked through with perspiration and blood. In the sickening heat, my vision swam. I could smell the crème brulee smell of burning sugarcane.

The parking lot of the shopping center where they'd taken me was empty, save for the rental car and one other darkened car that sat about 25 yards away under the piling for one of the sodium lights.

A beat passed. Then another.

Hamhocks looked to Surfer Dude and then back to me. He shrugged.

"Might as well get this over with," he said.

Surfer Dude nodded.

"Better if you close your eyes, pal," Hamhocks said, almost kindly. "It won't hurt -- much."

He pressed the barrel of the nine-millimeter to my temple.

"Wait," a woman's voice – hauntingly, shockingly familiar said. "He deserves to know why."

A ghostly, strawberry-blonde apparition stepped from the shadows. My eyes widened in horror. I fought the urge to vomit.

"Lena," I said, the shock hitting me like a freight train. My stomach rebelled. My heart went into overdrive and I sank to the ground.

"You should have left well enough alone, Sean," she said, tears in her eyes. "I didn't want it to end like this."

"Why?" I asked her.

The front of Lena's shirt was stained with streaks of blood. I was filled with horror.

"Inez ..." I said.

Lena looked at me, almost sadly, then her eyes hardened.

"She was a complication," she said. "A complication that I had to take care of – because of you. The alligators will take care of the rest."

"Why?" I asked pointlessly. "I loved you – love you – how could you?" I said. My voice was hoarse and ragged. My throat felt like it was filled with glass. Every word was an ordeal.

Lena shrugged.

"You know what a press aide makes, Sean?" she asked. "It's nothing. There were months when I could barely make my rent. Clarence offered me a way out. He offered me things. In return ... I gave him certain things as well."

"Clarence?" I said, not recognizing the name for a moment. "Oh God, McGeehan? The senator?"

I couldn't fight it anymore. I vomited. Bile, mixed with blood, splashed onto the ground.

Lena shrugged. She held a cigarette in one hand. I didn't even know she smoked.

"A girl's got to do what a girl's got to do," she said, so matter-of-factly that she could have been talking about the weather. "Dinners. Vacations. Nice clothes. I liked the lifestyle."

"Did you love him?" I spat.

Lena laughed a hollow, hard laugh.

"Don't be ridiculous," she said. "Love's got nothing to do with it."

Her face softened.

"But you, Sean, you were different," she said, she leaned into me, stroking my face as she pushed sweaty tendrils of hair from my eyes.

"You," she whispered. "You ... you I loved."

The lump in my throat was huge.

"Then why, Lena? Why?"

"Because love isn't enough," she said. "Not for me."

She stood up, brushing gravel from her knees. She walked away from me and went to stand with my two, erstwhile executioners.

"Is that what happened to Peter Andre, too?" I asked her.

She practically spat her answer.

"Peter Andre was a distraction. And he was disgusting. He had no idea how to treat a lady."

"Hard to do when there isn't one around," I shot back. Lena's eyes flashed, she rushed to me and smacked me hard across the face. My cheek burned from the impact. But the pain of everything else far outweighed it.

"All you had to do was leave well enough alone. We could have been good together," she said. "I figured you would have gotten the message after that beating that landed you in the hospital. But you kept after it. Why couldn't you just leave it alone, Sean?"

"I'm funny that way," I said.

She was silent.

"You've been feeding McGeehan – or Rocco Giambone – all this time, haven't you?" I asked. "That's how they knew we were here. That's why we're here now."

Lena looked at me, maybe for the last time.

"All you had to do was leave it alone, Sean," she said. She turned away from me and stepped into the shadows.

"Fuck it," she said to Hamhocks. "Get it done."

Hamhocks stepped forward again.

"Time's up, buddy," he said. "At least you know now."

The air filled with a huge explosion, and Hamhocks' head disappeared in a sickening red burst. I was covered by something wet that added to the stink of blood and perspiration that already coated me down to the bone.

Hamhocks fell over. His body landed on the pavement with a thud. His body twitched twice and then he was still.

Lena and Surfer Dude dived behind the rental car, searching frantically for the source of the gunfire. I threw myself forward onto the pavement.

Since my arms were bound behind me, there was nothing to cushion the impact. Gravel bit into my cheek as I landed. I grunted in pain.

It was silent. I glanced sideways as far my limited peripheral vision would let me. The gunfire sounded like it had come from the darkened car under the sodium light.

Lena and Surfer Dude were behind the rental car. They were breathing hard. Lena's eyes were wide with fear.

"What the hell was that," she demanded. "Who followed us?"

"I don't know," Surfer Dude said. He clutched a revolver to his chest. Slowly, he peeked his head above the hood of the rental car.

The air filled with the sharp report of another round of gunfire. Surfer Dude fell to the pavement, blood gushing from his neck. He grasped helplessly at the wound. Lena, stared, paralyzed at the horror.

"What do I do?" she asked me.

I didn't have an answer for her. I looked away and tried to figure out how I was going to get out of this charnel house.

Lena looked at me.

"We can get out of here together, Sean," she said, grasping for one last opportunity. "You and me. We can go someplace. I have money. We can get away together."

She ran to me and untied me.

I pulled myself, unsteadily, to my feet.

"You look awful," she said.

"I feel worse," I said. "But I think you'll probably feel worse in the morning."

"Why?" she asked.

I saw Lena eyeing Surfer Dude's gun, which sat just a few feet away from her on the pavement. I caught the glance and sidestepped quickly to the gun, snatched it from the pavement, and cocked it.

"Don't Lena," I said. "Don't even dream it."

She lunged at me. I had no choice. I hit her with the butt of the gun. There was a horrible, soft wet noise. She slumped to the pavement.

I listened for a long moment until I heard the steady intake of her breath.

In the distance, I saw Marty Herman approaching from the darkened parked car. He closed the distance in a moment. We could both hear the sirens.

He held out his hand. I shook it and then collapsed into him as my knees went weak from strain, fear and the searing pain in my chest.

"You gonna be all right?" he asked.

I pulled myself up and wiped still more of the blood from my forehead with the back of my hand. I looked at the bodies of the fallen gunnies and Lena, unconscious, on the pavement.

"I doubt it," I told him.

He nodded and we stood there in the sticky-hot night and waited for the cops to show up.

CHAPTER 38

The questioning by the local cops took the rest of the night.

They put Marty Herman and I in separate rooms and went up one side of us and down the other for hours. Through it all, my story never changed. There was nothing to lie about.

It was just the sad tale of a guy who had been taken for a ride.

That was something Peter Andre and I had in common. The only difference was that I was alive – just about – and he was dead.

At mid-morning, the cops gave us breakfast and a nurse came in to take care of my injuries. She cleaned the wounds and bandaged them with brisk efficiency.

"You're very lucky, you know," she told me, as she swabbed my forehead with rubbing alcohol. I winced and involuntarily pulled away.

"Sit still," she said. "This could have come out a lot worse."

"I know," I said hoarsely, taking a pull from the bottle of water that sat on the table in the conference room where they'd stashed me.

"Where's my friend?" I asked.

"The other police officer?" the nurse asked. She pulled a plastic bandage from her first-aid kit and stretched it across the cut on my forehead. I felt like crap. They'd cleaned my face up. But I was in my same clothes and I desperately wanted a shower.

"Uh-huh," I said.

"He's down the hall in another conference room. Professional courtesy, don't you know? He's doing fine. I think the two of you will be out of here soon."

She pulled off a pair of latex gloves and dropped them in a wastebasket.

"Good as new," she said as she inspected me.

"Really?"

She cocked her head to one side and gave me a grin.

"Well, almost," she said. "You could use a shower."

"Tell me about it," I said.

"Take care, dear," the nurse said, as she left, trailing a cloud of antiseptic and strong perfume in her wake.

"You too," I said to the door that closed behind her.

A few minutes later, a big cop, named Halloran, came into the room.

He hooked a chair from the table, turned it around, and sat down facing me.

"Let's go over this one more time," he said.

And we did.

It was past noon by the time they sprung us. Marty Herman and I met each in a corridor as we were let out of our respective conference rooms.

He looked like he'd been packed flat and folded wet. His eyes were red from sleeplessness and he wore a cross expression.

"You all right?" he asked, as two patrol cops rocked on the balls of their feet, waiting for us to be done.

"About as much as can be expected," I said.

"They're not gonna charge us with anything," he said. "I spent some quality time talking to the local district attorney. There was an imminent threat to your safety. And they concluded that I had the right to use deadly force."

I nodded.

"You gonna get into trouble?" I asked him.

Marty Herman barked a short laugh.

"Let's just say I'll have some explaining to do when I get home," he said.

"Sorry about that," I said.

"Comes with the territory," Marty said. And we walked down a long hallway past the empty squad-room and two more interview rooms to the front of the police station.

The walls were painted a pale yellow and there was the standard drop ceiling lined with fluorescent lights. It looked like any cop shop on earth. It had all the charm of a middle school.

As we walked down another long hallway, we passed Lena. She was sitting on a bench.

One ankle was handcuffed to a leg of the bench. She looked very small.

And it seemed as if that thing that had animated her, that tranquil beauty that I had fallen in love with, was gone.

She looked up as we approached. There was a look of infinite sadness in her eyes. My throat tightened and my chest felt heavy.

"Sean," she said, reaching a hand to me as we passed.

Trying very hard not to let the jumble of emotions welling in me spill out, I cast one, last sidelong glance at Lena, and passed without saying anything.

Behind me, I could hear a dry sob, and I glanced back a final time to see Lena's head resting on her knees, her shoulders heaving with sobs.

Involuntarily, I made to return to her. But Marty Herman put a heavy hand on my arm.

"Leave it, Sean," he said softly but forcefully. "There's nothing you can do for her now."

We kept walking

"What's going to happen to her?" I asked as we made it to the lobby.

"Don't know," Marty said. The two patrol cops who were escorting us were aggressively indifferent to the scene playing out before them. Marty turned and looked at them.

"You two got any idea?" he asked.

One of the patrolmen, a tall guy with a pock-marked face.

"Sarge said she was booked for murder," he said. "Murder?" I repeated.

The tall cop nodded.

"Sarge said she killed some Hispanic woman and dumped her body in a canal," he said. "Sick. Just sick. You know her?" He looked at me as he asked.

"Thought I did," I said.

"Humph," the tall cop said. We were in the lobby, standing at a long counter.

"You two are free to go," he said, handing us two manila

envelopes filled with our personal effects. I dumped the contents of mine onto the counter. Then I tucked my wallet and hotel key into my pants. My cell phone was gone. The two bruisers probably took it when they grabbed me.

Marty Herman grabbed up his stuff.

"Thanks," he said to the tall cop.

"Anything for a cop," he said. "But I hope we don't see you two here again."

"Don't worry," I said, "You won't."

He nodded quickly and then went back into the station, his younger partner trailing behind him.

Marty Herman and I went through the double doors of the police station and into a blazing hot south Florida sun.

"Cops said the car would be right down here," he said. We took a left out of the police station and walked half a block to an impound lot.

"There it is," Marty said, he jerked his head in the direction of a dark sedan with our hotel's name embossed on the side of it.

"You took one of their airport shuttles?" I asked. "I'm impressed."

Marty made a palms-up gesture with his hands.

"Didn't have any choice," he said. "I'd already parked the rental car and was walking back to the room when the heavies rushed past you and threw you into the back of the rental car. I had the keys, so I assume they wired it to get you out of there. I accosted one of the bellhops, explained my situation and flashed my badge. It was pretty easy."

My eyes widened.

"Wow," I said. "Resourceful. Maybe you'll finally make sergeant after all."

Marty Herman grunted. He unlocked the door to the hotel car and climbed inside.

"I'll be lucky if they don't' suspend me," he said.

"I can always be a character witness," I told him. "Tell them how you bravely saved a reporter from a fate worse than death."

Marty looked at me wryly.

"Sean, shut the fuck up and get in the car," he said.

And I did.

CHAPTER 39

We flew home from the West Palm Beach airport the next morning.

"Why's everyone staring at me?" I asked Marty as we walked through the terminal. We stopped at a magazine stand, where I bought a copy of that morning's Palm Beach Post.

Halfway through the local section, there was a small story about a violent incident at a shopping center just over the county line. My name wasn't mentioned.

Marty shrugged.

"Because you look like you just went 12 rounds with Tyson and lost – badly," he said. "Apart from that, you look great."

"Mmm," I said, studying the newspaper as we found two seats in the departure lounge.

I stretched my legs and dove into the newspaper. After all these years, it was still one of my favorite things to do.

Sure, I dug the Web and all. But for my money, there's still nothing like paging through and stumbling across a story you never expected.

Marty got up and returned a few minutes later with two, big cups of coffee. He handed me sugars and creamer. I dumped two each into my coffee.

He took his black.

"Thanks," I said. The coffee felt good.

The night before, we'd celebrated our good luck with barbecued shrimp and Red Stripe beer at this little place along the water that the hotel concierge had told us about.

Well, maybe good luck was too strong a word to describe where we were at the moment.

But the fact was, the sun was up, and I was alive. Even if my head was killing me and there was a jagged hole where my heart used to be. It was some-thing.

They soon called our flight, and Marty and I trudged aboard the flight to Charlotte. We'd catch a connector from there to Harrisburg. We were bumped and jostled as we squeezed down the aisle of the plane by oversized tourists with oversized bags that they tried to jam into undersized cargo compartments above their seats.

There was enough flowered material to reupholster a thousand sofas and enough hot air from the heavy breathing of the tourists to power a small Kansas town. When had air travel become so unglamorous?

Marty and I settled into a pair of seats. I took the aisle, and repeatedly had my shoulders bruised by passing pachyderms.

"You ever think that airlines are God's revenge for figuring out how to fly?" I asked him.

Marty stifled a laugh.

A flight attendant, struggling mightily to contain a grin, overheard my remark.

"You don't know the half of it," she said.

"Maybe you could tell me about it sometime," I told her.

She smiled a dazzling smile, displaying lots of white, very even teeth.

"Maybe I could," she said, resting one tanned hand on my shoulder, and went back to work.

Marty gave me a congratulatory punch on my right arm.

"Already getting back into the game," he said.

"Ehh ... maybe," I told him.

I fell asleep not long after the plane took off. Some people have trouble sleeping on planes, but I never have.

The flight attendant, the one with the dazzling smile, shook me awake as she served the drink service.

"Something to drink, sir?" she asked, as she put down a napkin and an impossibly small package of peanuts. I asked her for a Diet Coke.

To my amazement, she left the entire can.

"I think she likes you," Marty said, taking a pull from his $9 bottle of Budweiser.

"Maybe," I said, and pulled the napkin up to wipe my mouth.

As I drew it closer, I saw impeccably neat handwriting on the other side. I grinned and showed it to Marty.

He laughed.

I smiled to myself and tucked the napkin with the flight attendant's name, e-mail address and telephone number on it into my pocket.

We changed planes in Charlotte and made it home to Harrisburg by nightfall. Soft snow was falling when Marty Herman and I said goodbye under a portico leading to the baggage claim.

"Thank you, Marty," I said. "For everything."

Marty Herman pulled his coat tightly about him. The falling snowflakes refracted the light. The sky had that purple color it always has during a good snowfall, and everything was quiet.

Behind us, I could hear a plane taking off. I watched as the giant metal beast blasted past the gleaming white monolith of the terminal. But even the roar of its engines seemed muffled by the snow.

"You're welcome, Sean," he said. "But I'm sorry as hell that it had to end the way it did. I liked Lena. I really did."

I waved a hand as if trying to swat away the memory. I was lying to myself and I knew it.

"It's nothing," I said. "I'll get over it."

"Will you?" Marty asked as he shouldered his bag when a taxi approached.

"Maybe," I told him, walking with him to the cab. The cabbie rushed from the driver's seat and around the car to open the door for him.

"Where to, sir?" he asked in heavily accented English. He was short and wearing a newsboy's flat cap on his head.

"Harrisburg," Marty said. "Second and Division Street."

Marty handed his bag to the cabbie.

"Share a ride?" he asked me.

I shook my head.

"My car's in the long-term lot," I said. "I've got to wait for the shuttle."

"Suit yourself," Marty said as he climbed into the cab. I closed the door behind him.

"Take care, Marty," I said through the open window.

Marty Herman reached a gloved hand through the cab's window.

We shook hands, staring each other hard in the eye. I could feel the warmth of the cab's heater blowing through the opened window, warming my face in the cold night. The force of it blew my hair out of my eyes.

"You too, Sean," he said. "You too."

The cab pulled away from the curb and I was alone with the softly falling snow. I got my car and drove home through the purple darkness.

When I got home, I collected up the unopened mail that had collected in my vestibule.

My house had a closed in, overheated smell to it.

Though it was cold out, I opened one of the living room windows that looked out over Race Street and the river. The cold air blew in from the river and took away some of the stuffiness.

I threw the junk mail into the trash as I poured myself two fingers of Irish whiskey from a bottle in the kitchen. I added a few cubes of ice from the freezer and sat the glass down to let the ice melt a little bit and dilute the whiskey.

The bills that had amassed while I was away went into a nook above my desk. And that's when I saw it.

One of my old R.E.M. tour t-shirts was draped over the back of my desk chair. I picked it up and smelled it. There was a lingering scent of Lena's citrus perfume. I pulled the t-shirt close to me, rubbing it against my face.

It was like having a scab pulled off. I knew I shouldn't have done it, but I did anyway. And I searched for one good memory of her.

I couldn't find one. I might eventually, I knew. But I couldn't yet. I took the t-shirt into the kitchen and dropped it into the sink. I took a book of matches from a drawer and struck one.

The match caught the edge of the t-shirt and I stood there a long time, drinking whiskey and watching the shirt burn.

When it was done, I ran water over the scraps and dumped the charred remnants of the shirt into the garbage.

I walked into my living room to the stereo. I found Miles Davis' "Kind of Blue," in my CD collection and pushed it into the tray of the CD player. I hit play and listened to the opening strains of "So What?"

I sat back on my couch and let Miles' music wash over me. I'd brought the bottle of whiskey into the room with me, and when my glass was empty, I filled it up again. My feet were propped up on the coffee table, and I rested my head on the back of the couch and closed my eyes.

"This one's for you, Miles," I said, proposing a toast to my silent room.

Not for the first time, and not for the last, I fell asleep in my clothes.

CHAPTER 40

When I woke up, the sun was streaming through my living room window and my tongue was stuck to the roof of my mouth.

My head felt like it was stuffed full of cotton and my skin felt gritty.

I stripped in my living room and threw the clothes in the trash.

It seemed wasteful, but I didn't want them anymore. My jeans were stained with dirt and blood.

The shirt I'd picked up in a bargain shop near the hotel? I could live without it.

I wanted the stain of Florida off me.

Upstairs, I turned up the shower as hot as I could stand it, and then I stood there for a long time under the water and thought about where the last year had brought me.

My thoughts were hardly linear, like those reminisces so often are. My thoughts dashed from event to event to event, and then back again.

I thought about Peter Andre and that car crash on Cameron Street all those months ago and how he'd been spotted with a blonde-haired woman I now knew to be Lena.

Lena ... my stomach got tight at the thought of her.

I held onto the wall of the shower, and, for the first time since that night in Florida, I let the tears come. I cried silently for a few minutes in the shower, letting the hot water run over me, mixing with the tears until I hoped I had washed them – and her – away.

And then I thought about Rocco Giambone and the Greater Doylestown Development Corporation and Oscar Veracruz and Sunshine Properties and the parcel of land in suburban Philadelphia and the holding company that owned it, Independence Partners.

I thought about all this a little more while I shaved. I stared at my reflection in the bathroom mirror. Most of the swelling was gone from my face. There were still two nasty shiners around each eye, but those were beginning to fade.

I dried my hair and got dressed, thinking some more about what I knew.

I pulled on clean jeans, a white t-shirt and an old gray sweatshirt that I'd had since my twenties. It was worn and comfortable and fit me like a second skin. I slid into a pair of vintage Adidas Stan Smith tennis shoes and went downstairs.

I had a bowl of cereal for breakfast and watched the morning news on MSNBC.

I made a pot of coffee and rummaged all the Peter Andre paperwork – the piles of campaign finance reports and documents, along with the card signed in the neat, loping female hand that had started it all.

I looked at the card for a long time and sat it on top of my desk.

I poured myself a cup of coffee, added sugar and cream, and fired up my computer.

And then I did what I do best – I wrote, piecing it all together, piece by painstaking piece.

And then, when I felt like I'd gotten to a good place, where I thought I had my case in order, I hit print and I went to see state Senator J. Clarence McGeehan.

CHAPTER 41

State Senator J. Clarence McGeehan's suite of offices on the third floor of the Capitol were still painted in the same muted shade of blue as when I'd last visited.

His staff was just as quietly deferential and efficient, and as I closed the pebbled glass door behind me, I could hear his stentorian voice booming somewhere from within the suite of offices.

Two aides hurried out of a doorway. Their faces were shaded with equal measures of fear and relief at having escaped.

I presented myself to the receptionist.

It was Estella, the woman who had greeted me the last time I was here. She was still olive-skinned. But this time, the stiff blonde highlights were gone. And her hair had reverted to its natural jet black.

Estella's face was framed by ringlets of tight, dark curls that gleamed in the light of the office.

"Remember me, Estella," I said, as I greeted her.

Estella, looked up, her face momentarily frozen in surprise.

"Of course, Mister ... ahh ... Flynn, isn't it?" she asked. "How can I help you today?"

When I looked down, I saw for the first time that Estella's belly was swollen behind the desk. She was pregnant.

She followed my glance and her face broke into a wide grin.

"I know," she said, cradling her stomach. "I'm huge."

"How far along are you?" I asked.

"Nearly eight months," she said. "I can't wait. It's my first."

"You know what you're having?" I asked.

"A boy," she grinned and nodded. "Now, again, Mister Flynn, what can I do for you today?"

"Oh, right," I said. "Sorry. I'm here to see Senator McGeehan."

Estella clicked a few keys on her computer keyboard and a calendar flashed up on the screen.

"Do you have an appointment, Mister Flynn?" she asked. "I don't see one here."

"No, I don't," I said quickly. "And, Estella, it's Sean. Please call me Sean."

"Of course," she said. "The senator is very busy this afternoon. I don't know if he'll have time to talk to you."

I shook my head emphatically.

"What I need to talk to him about won't take long," I said. "Can you get me in for five or ten minutes?"

Estella frowned, biting her bottom lip.

She clicked a few more keys, moving some appointments around on the calendar.

"Let me see what I can do," Estella said.

She disappeared into the suite of offices and a few seconds later, I could hear McGeehan's voice booming again. Estella re-emerged from the rear of the suite. Her face was pale.

"I'm sorry, Sean," she said. "He just doesn't have time to see you. And ... umm ... he's in a bit of a mood today."

I nodded. And then my mouth hardened to a thin line.

"Tell him I want to talk to him about Independence Partners and Oscar Veracruz. Tell him I've spent some time in West Palm Beach recently."

Estella gave me a blank look.

"I don't understand," she said.

"Tell him, Estella," I said. "Please."

She sighed heavily.

"All right, for you, just this once," she said. "But I warn you, if I go into early labor, it's your fault."

I put my hands up in a gesture of mock surrender. "Yes, ma'am," I said.

Estella went back into McGeehan's office. I heard the booming voice. Then, it stopped abruptly.

Estella came back out to me, a baffled look on her face.

"The senator will see you now," she said.

"That's what I thought," I said without humor. Then, to Estella, I added, "If I'm not back in an hour, call the Capitol Police."

She looked at me quizzically.

McGeehan, still ageless and white-haired, was seated behind his desk when I came in. He was staring at a liquid- crystal computer monitor. From where I was standing, it looked as if the screen was filled with legalese.

"You've got five minutes, Flynn," he said. He didn't ask me to sit, so I sat down in one of the wing chairs across from his desk.

One of McGeehan's snowy white eyebrows climbed up his forehead in irritation, but he didn't say anything.

"It's over for you, you know," I said, taking a notebook from my back pocket.

"And just what is that?" he asked, his voice still patrician, but colored by a note of tension.

"You already know," I said. "Or you wouldn't have agreed to see me."

"It's not what you think," he said. McGeehan rose from his desk and walked to a long window that looked out over the North Street side of the Capitol.

Outside, last night's snow had coated the grounds. But it was gray and plowed under in places from where the state trucks had cleared it away.

"I've got a really tough re-election campaign coming up this year," he said quietly.

"So?" I asked. "That a good enough reason to get involved with scum like Veracruz and take his money?"

McGeehan was silent.

"Or his women?" I asked, anger rising in my throat like a tide. I thought about Guadalupe Guerra.

Marty and I called the Sarasota cops before we left. They'd shut down Sunshine Properties, and Guadalupe was on her way home, back to her family in El Salvador. But she'd never see her sister again.

His back to me, McGeehan stiffened. I saw his shoulders rise.

"That's right," I said. "I know about the women. And I know you liked them. Christ ... they're young enough to be your granddaughters."

"I'm old," McGeehan said futilely. "I'm lonely."

"And when I got to West Palm, Veracruz was keeping them in a fucking meth lab."

I walked over to McGeehan and spun him around.

"And because I found out about your little arrangement, it got someone killed," I boomed at him, my nose only inches from his. The color drained from his face.

"Is that worth re-election, senator?" I asked. "Is the life of a twenty-three-year-old woman worth your re-election?" McGeehan seemed to deflate before me.

"I rationalized it," he said. "I figured if I took Veracruz's money, I could channel it into something good. It did pay for good things, you know."

"Through the Greater Doylestown Development Corporation?" I asked.

McGeehan nodded.

"Where Veracruz laundered his drug money," I said. It wasn't a question.

McGeehan nodded again.

"The money paid for a playground, you know," he said.

"I don't care," I said. "That money had blood on it."

McGeehan shook his head. "I didn't know," he said.

"Bullshit," I fired back. "You knew exactly what you were doing. That's why you and Veracruz bought that property in Solebury. That's why you ramrodded that tax break through the General Assembly."

McGeehan sank into one of the leather-upholstered chairs that ringed the conference table where we'd met for the first time all those months before.

"For God's sake, you were going to give a drug dealer and a pimp a tax break on the backs of the people of this state just so you could ensure your re-election," I said. "Am I right?"

McGeehan didn't say anything. The fight was out of him now.

"The money does good in the community," he said. "I thought I might be able to help those young ladies."

"Oh, balls," I said. "You weren't thinking about helping anyone but yourself. And now that you're nailed, you're sorry. Christ, you fucking people are all the same."

McGeehan's eyes flashed at the profanity.

He wasn't used to being talked to that way. It was a safe bet that no one had told him "no" for years because they were afraid of what would happen to them.

"And my guess is that Peter Andre found out about all of this, confronted you, and threatened to blow the whistle," I said. "Probably was gonna go to the Attorney General. Working for you, he probably put together the paper trail. The same one I followed to get to you."

McGeehan said nothing as he contemplated the magnitude of his ruin. He looked very old and very tired. And I didn't care. "That's right, Senator," I said. "I've got all the paper – all of it – and I can tie you and Giambone to Veracruz, and Lena confessed everything to me in Florida just before she tried to kill me."

"Please don't," McGeehan said, his eyes had a plea in them now. "My career will be over. I'm a Pennsylvania state senator."

"You don't deserve the title," I said. "The story runs tomorrow. Anything you want to say?"

McGeehan laughed a harsh little laugh. It sounded like it came from some dark place inside him.

"No comment," he said and then turned away.

By Sean Flynn and Michael Vivian Banner Staff Writers
HARRISBURG _ A Philadelphia-area state senator abruptly resigned his seat yesterday after being confronted with the results of a Banner investigation that concluded he used his power and prestige to secure tax breaks for a suspected drug dealer.

Sen. J. Clarence McGeehan, a 30-year legislative veteran, and chairman of the Senate Appropriations Committee declined to comment when he was presented with the results of a six-month investigation by The Banner.

Through interviews and documents, the newspaper was able to conclude that McGeehan, 62; Harrisburg political consultant Rocco Giambone, 59; and a Florida man, Oscar Veracruz, conspired to launder drug profits through a Bucks County non-profit jointly run by Giambone and McGeehan's chief-of-staff, Larry J. Keller, 61, of Doylestown, Bucks County. Documents showed that Veracruz, 41, of Wellington, Fla., used his business, Sunshine Properties, to make donations to the non-profit, the Greater Doylestown Development Corporation. Giambone, who also runs a Harrisburg-area political action committee, is listed as one of the group's officers, documents showed.

In turn, the non-profit made donations to the Giambone-operated Better Government Association of Pennsylvania, which has offices in the 200 block of State Street.

Giambone declined repeated requests for comment and released a statement through his lawyer asserting his innocence. Records obtained from the Pennsylvania Department of State show that the PAC, in turn, made more than a half-million dollars in contributions to McGeehan's re-election campaign committee over the last five years.

A spokesman for the state Attorney General's office said the agency had initiated a probe of McGeehan's non-profit, Giambone's PAC and Veracruz's relationship to both men.

In addition, the Palm Beach County sheriff's office said it had charged a Democratic state Senate aide, Lena Bergstrom, 27, of Harrisburg, with first-degree murder in connection with the stabbing death of a 23-year-old woman in Wellington, Fla.

According to an arrest report, Bergstrom claimed she had acted at the behest of McGeehan's top aide, Frank Schildner, 50, of Camp Hill, Cumberland County. In a statement to investigators, Bergstrom also implicated McGeehan, Veracruz, and Giambone in the death last summer of McGeehan aide Peter Andre, 26, of Elizabethtown, Lancaster County.

Ed Stanley, a spokesman for the Attorney General's Office, said Bergstrom's statements had been handed over to Harris-

burg city police, which is handling that portion of the investiga-
tion.

sean.flynn@bannernews.com (717)885-6628

EPILOGUE

A week later, I was standing at my kitchen counter watching the Pittsburgh Penguins lose badly to Boston on my DVR when the mail cascaded through the mail-slot in my front door.

I was having a late breakfast. I'd been out late with a few friends the night before toasting my success.

The story about McGeehan's ties to a drug ring in Florida and his role in the death of his young aide, Peter Andre, had sparked a probe by the state Attorney General's office.

A grand jury was to be convened later in the month and McGeehan was telling anyone and everyone who would listen that the Banner had libeled him and that he was going to sue me and all my descendants.

I probably would have been nervous were it not for the fact that the newspaper's lawyers had spent hours vetting my story, prompting hours of careful editing, and more editing, before the story was in publishable shape.

But it finally ran.

And when it did, it blew the lid off Harrisburg in a way that hadn't been seen for quite a while.

The television stations picked it up. And it even made national news.

What made the victory sweetest of all was not the fact that I'd helped bring down a powerful figure. No, McGeehan was the architect of his own fate.

It was the fact that, just like in Watergate, the story had been broken by a cops reporter, not the political reporter who was so plugged into the pulse of Capitol Hill.

That was satisfying. And it was nice to know, that even after all these years, I could still pull off the big story when the occasion called for it.

Of course, it wasn't all sweetness and light. Melanie Goslin got stuck writing the story about Lena, and how she was facing twin murder charges in Pennsylvania and Florida for the deaths of Peter Andre and Inez Guerra.

There was no joy in that at all. There never would be any.

I brought the mail back to my kitchen counter, tossed the junk mail into the garbage and put the bills into a place by themselves so I could ignore them later.

There was a copy of that week's issue of the New Republic and Sports Illustrated.

At the bottom of the stack was a postcard. It had a picture of the state Capitol on the front of it and a Harrisburg postmark. There was just one sentence written across the back: "Thank you for not giving up," it read. It was written in a neat, female hand.

It reminded me of something I needed to do.

It was a Tuesday morning, and I was taking my time getting into work. I picked up the phone and dialed.

"I think we should meet," I said. "Kunkel Plaza – half an hour."

I hung up, finished my breakfast and put on my coat and shoes. The Penguins would just have to wait.

Thirty minutes later, I was at Kunkel Plaza along the river at the base State Street where it terminated at the Susquehanna River.

I was standing near the bench that contained one of the city's most famous sculptures – a brass carving of a man in a business suit reading a newspaper. My back was to the Capitol and I was looking out over the river.

It was frozen in places, and through the cracks in the ice, I could see the brown water flowing down to the Chesapeake Bay and then to the sea.

After a few minutes, I felt a presence beside me. I looked up. Estella DiMartino, McGeehan's assistant, stood next to me.

"Can we sit down?" she asked, gesturing to a nearby stone bench.

I squinted against the pale gray of the sky. A cold wind blew in from the river.

"It was you," I said. "You were the one who sent me the package telling me to follow the money all those months ago."

I looked at Estella's belly, big with the child she would soon bear.

"Now I know why I was sent it," I said. "And now I know who sent it."

She sat silently next to me and stared out at the river.

"It's what my baby deserves," she said. "Someday, I want to be able to tell him about his father and tell him that he died trying to do the right thing, that he wasn't one for taking the easy way out. My baby will know the truth."

"That's a good thing to do," I told her.

"It's the only thing to do," she said. "Thank you, Sean."

And then we were both quiet, staring out at the river, letting it take us both out to sea.

An award-winning political journalist with more than 25 years' experience in the news business, **John L. Micek** is the Editor-in-Chief of **The Pennsylvania Capital-Star**, a Harrisburg, Pa. based, nonpartisan, nonprofit news site dedicated to honest and aggressive coverage of Pennsylvania state government, politics and policy.

Before joining the **Capital-Star**, **Micek** spent six years as Opinion Editor at **PennLive/The Patriot-News** in Harrisburg, Pa., where he helped shape and lead a multiple-award-winning Opinion section for one of Pennsylvania's most-visited news websites.

Prior to that, he spent 13 years covering Pennsylvania government and politics for **The Morning Call** of Allentown, Pa. His career has also included stints covering Congress, Chicago City Hall and more municipal meetings than he could ever count.

Micek contributes regular analysis and commentary to a host of broadcast outlets, including **CTV News** in Canada and **talkRadio** in London, U.K., as well as "*Face the State*" on **CBS-21** in Harrisburg, Pa.; "*Pennsylvania Newsmakers*" on **WGAL-8** in Lancaster, Pa., and the **Pennsylvania Cable Network**. His weekly column on American politics is syndicated nationwide to more than 800 newspapers by **Cagle Syndicate**.

He lives in suburban Harrisburg with his wife and daughter.